CW00743199

# Mr Tim

Peter George

cffoip

Copyright © Peter George 2012.

The right of Peter George to be identified as author of this Book
has been asserted by him in accordance with the
Copyright, Designs & Patents Act 1988

All rights reserved. No part of this publication may be reproduced,
stored in a retrieval system or transmitted in any form or by any
means without the prior written permission of the publisher, nor be
otherwise circulated in any form of binding or cover other than that in
which it is published and without a similar condition including this
condition being imposed on the subsequent purchaser.

This book is a work of fiction. People, places, events and situations are
the product of the author's imagination. Any resemblance to actual
persons, living or dead, places or historical events, is purely
coincidental.

ISBN 978-0-9530062-1-2

First published by Peter George in 2012
Carn Ffoi Publications
Trellys, Mountain West,
Newport
Pembrokeshire
SA42 0QX

Set in Raleigh Serial

Printed and bound in the UK by Witley Press, Hunstanton, Norfolk

Cover design and artwork by Leon Olin & Sylvia Gainsford

**Also published as an ebook - find it on amazon kindle store**

## About the Author

Peter George grew up in West Wales, is married with three children and three grand-children. Now retired and living on a hill in Pembrokeshire he is a member of The Society of Authors, The Performing Rights Society and an associate member of Literature Wales. He was awarded a Hawthornden Fellowship in 2010.

## BY THE SAME AUTHOR

*Novels*
Undreamed Shores

*Poetry*
Ceredigion Cycle and Other Poems
Antiphony of a Grief Rewarded
Adam the Man
Four eyes – (Joint collection with the late Peter Heneker Ksg)

In memory of MM

## Acknowledgements

I am grateful to my wife and my children for their patience and encouragement; also Stephanie, Margaret, Wendy, Sue, Vivien, Frances, Flora and Bryan for reading and George for much needed technical help. Special thanks to Leon & Sylvia for the work of art which is the front cover. The first draft of this book was written at Hawthornden Castle Retreat for Writers thanks to the grant of a Hawthornden Fellowship in 2010 without which this book might not have been written.

# CHAPTER 1

Tim Barrington-Lewis parted the lace curtains and peered out of his bedroom window. His beery night with Rhydian and James still lingered in the aching voids above his eyes. He pulled at the sash; then banged it open. He took a deep breath, hoping it might do him some good and shivered. The air was cold for October and smelling unmistakeably of cow. The yard below was bright with overnight rain. Opposite stood a sway-backed range of moss-covered stone buildings which seemed to have been fashioned by nature, not man. A large oak tree, its wet leaves streaming in the wind and pirouetting to the ground one by one, grew out of a stone bank. Tim shut the window, returned to the washstand and poured hot water from a jug into a large, green bowl. He examined himself in the mirror which hung on long cords, half of its silver gone and cursed. The shig which, last night, was a mere pimple had now erupted into its full, crimson glory. The damned things had been a problem since prep school. There it had meant dodging matron whose panacea, a livid gentian violet, had left you with a face like a baboon's bottom for the rest of term. He would have to cover it up somehow. He reached for his razor. When he had dressed, Tim looked about him. The room smelt of size and new wallpaper, its relentless lines of red roses running up to an uneven ceiling. Apart from the single bed with dark wooden ends the only other pieces of furniture were a brown, rexine armchair and a wooden bedside cabinet. On the far wall hung a picture in murky browns and greens. Above the bed-head was a sampler instructing him to 'pray without ceasing.'

The staircase led down to a large kitchen with a flagstone floor and an open fireplace you could stand under, sheltering a blaze of logs in a broad, iron basket. To the left of the fire stood a curving, high-backed settle. Tim stood with his back to the fire, looking up at the gaping void of the flue where the smoke curled on its way to the chimney. The place seemed to be welcoming and, better still, it smelt of bacon. There was no one about but he could hear voices. ... A door to the right of the stairs opened.

'I hope that you slept well, Mr Barrington-Lewis.'

'Yes, thank you, Mrs Evans;' the bed had creaked, the mattress was lumpy and the pillow hard – like school dorms but Tim did not wish to upset the broad, homely, apron-clad woman who was smiling at him; 'and please call me Tim.' ...

'Beth,' she cried, turning her head, 'come and meet the gentleman.'

A young woman, looking flustered and tying an apron around her long skirt, appeared in the doorway and bobbed at Tim.

'My daughter is very excited that you are coming to stay with us; aren't you Beth? ... Now take the gentleman through to the parlwr bach. We mustn't keep him waiting for his breakfast.'

As Tim followed he reckoned that Beth wasn't bad-looking, her raven hair trailing down the milk-white complexion of her neck and on to her back, in coils. She turned right off a corridor into a small room with a table laid for one over a starched, white cloth. In a corner a glass-fronted cabinet displayed china that Mother would have thrown out. The place smelt of damp. …

'Mam thinks you will be cosy here,' said Beth.

'Could I eat in the kitchen?'

'With us?'

'Yes… with you.'

'I hope Mam won't mind,' said Beth, her face flushing. … 'It will be like having another brother,'

'You have a brother?'

'Yes, Geraint.'

'Where is he?'

'Out with the cows… and I've got a sister; Lowri's older than me … and she's got babies.'

'Then you're an aunt.'

'Yes… I'm an auntie. Isn't that nice?'…


Tim stood in the narrow hallway, admiring himself in a mirror which formed part of a coat stand. His new tweed jacket and plus fours, with matching socks and cap, looked good. He turned to leave, coming face to face with 'Mam' who touched him on his sleeve.

'I should have told you last night but it was late and I didn't and I don't want to say this to you in front of Beth,' Mam whispered. 'There's something under your bed … when you need it!'

Tim was feeling puzzled. 'What thing?'

Mam drew herself up and took a deep breath. 'Well … if,

at night, you were to have a call of …'

'You mean a chamber pot,' said Tim, his face beginning to redden.

'Yes,' Mam sighed with relief, 'and it's got a lid; and you don't have to do anything with it. Beth will check it every morning when she cleans your room.' …

The journey to Rhywle was a good five miles but the Morris Minor would make short work of it. The car was his pride and his freedom, having cost a sizeable chunk of what little remained of his trust money but well spent. Its perky motor was speeding him past green fields, lime-washed farmsteads and high hedges draped in the colours of autumn. He began to reflect upon Mrs Evans's instructions. … He would only use the pot in extremis and he was damned if he was going to let Beth or anyone else get involved. It could be bloody embarrassing – the problem being that he would have to get through the kitchen unnoticed to the one lavatory tacked on to the rear of the house. … He pulled up. The road ahead was unfamiliar. …

The office was an ageing, four-storey building at the centre of Rhywle where the few streets met to form a square. Tim entered 'reception,' an open space for customers, hemmed in by high-fronted desks, their occupants shielded by panelling in wood and glass. A buzz of conversation ceased. A girl popped her head above a screen and smirked at him. 'Are you Mr Barrington-Lewis?'

'Yes.'

'The Brigadier wants to see you.'

Tim anxiously consulted an antique clock on the wall above the desks. 'Where do I find him?'

'Upstairs; ... he's last on the left.' The head withdrew into a storm of giggling. ...

'You're late ... you bloody boy ... ten minutes late!' The Brigadier wasn't looking at him. He was making notes.

'I took a wrong turning, sir.'

An aged black dog with a silver-haired muzzle, lodged in the space between the two desk pillars, unwound itself, creaked into an upright position and snarled. The Brigadier banged the desktop, shouting 'Down Inca, down!' The animal sank gratefully back into the comfort of its wicker basket. The Brigadier straightened up and glared at Tim. 'The dog's got the answer to that. We don't have any excuses here, do we Inca?' He patted the top of the desk and the old dog sighed; ... 'and, if you want to make a land agent, you'll have to learn to get up in the morning.' Tim wanted to explain that he had indeed got up early but the Brigadier's piercing blue eyes, set deep into a lined and skeletal face, looked hostile. It was clear that he was only interested in outcomes. He produced a silver fob watch from his waistcoat pocket and stood up. 'You and I are due at the market. We have an appointment with pigs. No time to explain now.'...

In the gunmetal light of an October morning the market seemed a bleak place of grey hard-standings, tubular rails and corrugated sheds of varying sizes. Men with sticks fussed and shouted over cattle being herded into corrals. Some were poking sheep and pigs into pens. Others, in drab dustcoats and caps, stood alone – leaning on crooks, eying the livestock; or in groups locked in close conversation. There was, overall, a sense of expectation. Tim sniffed. The air seemed a cocktail of varying kinds of excrement. … Rhyd's suggestion that becoming a land agent amounted to a combination of rubbing shoulders with the aristocracy and getting drunk at a classy agricultural college seemed inaccurate but what did he know? … The Brigadier was striding purposefully towards a large, wooden shed, Tim trotting in his wake. The door was flung open. Four young women ceased their loud conversation and looked up. One of them was holding a nail file. 'Put that damned thing away,' barked the Brigadier, glaring at her, his expression questioning.

She looked down demurely and whispered. 'Eleri, sir.'

'Ah … yes …Ellery. Will you brief this young man?'

'Brief, sir?'

'Show him the ropes. He's clerking for me with the pigs in ten minutes so look sharp. … Where's my stick?' A long, forked stick was handed over the counter by one of the other girls. The Brigadier took it and left.

In a matter of minutes Eleri had explained the intricacies of auction sale records. It seemed fairly straightforward; the vendor's name already entered in each case together with number, breed and identity marks of  pigs – blue spot on back or red spot on rump and so on. All Tim had to do was enter the sale price of each lot as it happened together with the purchaser's name and address. His anxiety began to ebb in the current of the girl's homely and reassuring voice. When she had finished she handed him the bundle of sale sheets and said. 'It's easier when you get to know them. … You'll have to watch out for him though.'

'Who?' Tim asked, aware that the other girls were trying to hide their amusement.

'The Brigadier. He sells like a bull at a gate and don't expect him to remember any names.' …

Tim found the Brigadier hovering close to the pig-pens but not near enough to get into conversation with the grey men who had gathered in anticipation of his performance.

'Good! You're on time, Barrington…?'

'Lewis, sir.'

'Quite so. … Ready for battle then; … got all the pages?'

'Yes sir.' Tim sensed a tension in the Brigadier; something he shared; the anxiety of two actors about to take to the stage with a potentially hostile audience and without a script. The Brigadier pointed at an elderly, balding and hunch-backed man on the edge of the gathering crowd. 'He's the Runner.'

'Runner sir?' Tim could not imagine that such a man could ever run.

'Yes, he takes your completed sale sheets to the girls so that the bills are ready when the customers call; and some go as soon as they've bought. … Don't underestimate him. He never fails; and he knows just about all of em.' …. The Brigadier looked Tim up and down and continued. 'If you should ask me, you're somewhat overdressed for this party.'

'I didn't know what to expect, sir.'

'Anything here, boy; anything. … You'll probably have your smart shoes covered in excrement by the end of the day. At least they're the right colour.' With this the Brigadier swung round, headed for the crowd and, with surprising ease and the aid of his stick, clambered onto slatted duck-boards which could have been no more than one foot six inches wide and at least three feet off the ground. Tim followed him. The pens, divided by railings, were set either side of the boards and seemed to go on for ever. The Brigadier was waving his stick and calling for order. His lanky presence, towering over the crowd and clad in a weathered tweed jacket with elbows patched in leather, old khaki breeches, puttees and black boots, made an impressive sight. … Suddenly he bawled 'I've got a pig. Who wants my pigs?' This primitive mantra was repeated over and over, shamelessly mixing the singular with the plural, until the bidding came – subtle hand gestures, looks, winks and nods under caps which the Brigadier's sharp eyes seemed miraculously to pick up. Each elevation in the price was announced and repeated as a bare figure without verbal embellishment until the next. A sale would be made by the crash of the Brigadier's stick against the boards, narrowly missing the heads of vendors standing among their own stock. The Brigadier's technique, even to the inexperienced, seemed unsophisticated. There was none of the smooth talk, leisurely pace and clever reminders of what was for sale that Tim had encountered at the country house auctions he had attended with Mother; … but the selling was going fast; very fast. They were now at the sixth pen and Tim had kept up, thanks to the grey men recognising him as a novice and co-operating. As the crowd shifted to the seventh pen, during a brief spell in the cacophony, one of them leaned over the railings and whispered. 'You've got me down for the green spots in the last – John Thomas?'

Tim consulted his sale sheet for pen six. 'Yes … and the blue.'

'Bugger! I didn't buy those as well.' The selling had started again and the man was waving his big hands at the Brigadier who promptly took a bid off him.

'That was no bid,' yelled the man. 'I wouldn't be seen dead with those runts on my farm!'

The Brigadier stopped and glared down at him. 'And who the hell are you?'

'John Thomas; ... I'm here every week.' A ripple of laughter flowed from the grey men. The Brigadier paused before he replied. 'Well, John Thomas; you've interrupted my sale. What's it about?'

'Your clerk here has got me down for the whole of pen six!'

The Brigadier sighed. 'Don't you know your colours boy?'

A dread was settling over Tim. 'Yes sir; but they were all mixed up.'

'So we've sold some of em twice! For how many pens?'

'I couldn't say but, possibly, all of them, sir.'

'All six!' The Brigadier banged his stick against the pen side. 'Very well. Stop the sale. Will all buyers recheck their purchases with my clerk. I look for your co-operation. ... It is his first day.'

Tim's face was burning at this unwelcome reminder of his incompetence. Men were pressing in on him – muttering names, colours and pen numbers. He was crouching now; balancing the sale sheets on his knees and, in the utter confusion, his writing hand froze. He sensed someone above him and looked up. The Quasimodo frame of the runner was peering over his shoulder. 'Can you help me?' Tim pleaded. Without a word the man began to take over, matching the men to the lots and repeating details slowly to Tim whose writing hand began to move again. Soon they had details of all that was missing except in the first pen. The runner gathered up the sale sheets and whispered 'I am sure that I know the buyer but he has gone after the sheep, no doubt. We will find him soon enough.' The voice was unexpectedly cultured in the way of the Welsh when venturing into the less familiar territory of English. Tim stood up to thank him but the man was already lurching over the decking at a cracking pace in the direction of the office. Tim turned to the Brigadier who had, throughout, remained detached from a disagreeable procedure that had probably lasted only minutes but which had felt like hours and indicated that he was ready to go on.

When the selling was over Tim sought the earliest opportunity to apologise for messing up. The Brigadier was looking weary. He rubbed his brow and ran his fingers through the remains of his silver hair 'Bit of a baptism of fire for you, I suppose.'

'Yes sir.'

'When we're oversubscribed there can be up to three lots in each pen, don't you know.'

'That must be difficult.'

'It damn well is and, looking down at these blighters all dressed the same and mixed up with their pigs, it's hard to know who's who or what's what.'

Tim paused. This, he believed, was the closest he'd ever get to an admission of weakness from the Brigadier but it was, nevertheless, a welcome gesture.

'We were rescued by the runner,' continued the Brigadier, thoughtfully; 'he'd make a damned good sergeant if he could be straightened out.' Tim was pondering the impracticality of the Brigadier's suggestion and stifled a grin. The Brigadier interrupted his train of thought. 'Never judge anyone by first appearance; that's what I say.'

Tim looked down, taking this as an admonition. 'Of course sir.'

'You need a break. Have you a piece?'

'A what, sir?'

'A sandwich; a pie?'

'No sir.'

'How very improvident?' The Brigadier was scouring the depths of a pocket. 'On this occasion I'll let you have a share of mine.' He produced a wrinkled, brown paper bag, unwrapped it and peeled off a damp, compressed, white bread sandwich. 'Here, take this and don't forget to bring your own next time. ... Who are you with?'

'Pardon sir?'

'Who are you billeted with?'

'Mrs Evans of Penllan Farm.'

The Brigadier paused. 'Where's that?'

'Between here and Twll, sir.'

'Tiger country; back of beyond; ... you happy there?'

'Yes sir. It seems to be ... '

'Got to see someone; no time for conversation now,' snapped the Brigadier, cutting him short. 'Go and stand by the office and, by the way, we call it "the hut" round here because that is all it really is. You'll get picked up by Captain Thomas. You'll be selling store cattle with him from fourteen hundred hours.' The Brigadier stalked off; then checked, turned and bellowed; 'and remember to eat that sandwich.

11

You'll need it.'…

Boz had finished his morning's performance in the main ring. Heading for the hut in the company of Teg he was in confident mood, acknowledging shouted greetings from farmers and dealers alike with a wave and a smile. The selling of cattle always went well if the sun was shining and, in October, after overnight rain, it was a real tonic – putting people in a good mood; promising to shorten the winter. Sheep seemed to sell in any weather – the buyers, many of them hill farmers, well used to the wild conditions which so often frequented their upland pastures. …

Boz patted Teg on the shoulder.

*'Good thing you spotting that dodgy buyer, Teg.'*

*'He is a shifty sort of a man if you should ask me; … from away. You remember Miss Morgan had to put the lawyers on to him last time he bought.'*

Boz consulted his watch and looked towards the hut.

*'There he is; can't miss him – looking like a proper gent; and no boots! I'll have to keep him out of the cachi.'*

*'He's taller than us,'* said Teg.

*'It wouldn't take much to be taller than you, Teg.'*

Tim stood, considering the morning's events and fearing what the afternoon might bring. If hell could be conjured into a contemporary setting it would happily fit in here. He examined the sandwich, its corners already lifting in the growing heat of the sun. He sniffed at it. It stank of dead fish. He decided to experiment with one bite before the thing warmed up any more.

'Is that your lunch?' A red-faced, dapper man with dark, neatly groomed hair and laughing eyes, was pointing. 'What's in that? I can smell it from here.'

'I don't know,' said Tim, lifting a corner of soggy, white bread.

The man leaned forward, inspected the contents and sniffed. 'Ach y fi. Where did you get it?'

'From the Brigadier.'

'That explains everything.' The man took the sandwich and threw it into a bin behind them. 'He makes his own out of God knows what. ... It's a wonder he's still alive. Come on; I'll buy you a proper lunch.'

Tim hesitated. 'Are you Captain Thomas?'

'Yes ... but we're not at war now; everyone here calls me Boz; short for Boswell; and you're...?'

'Tim Lewis; ... Barrington-Lewis,' Tim replied, immediately regretting the use of his full surname in response to the other's apparent informality.

Whatever it was, it did not look like a restaurant; or a café even. No windows, no name, no signs outside inviting custom. Tim concluded that the place relied upon its reputation. He peered through the low door into a dark and steamy interior which smelt of spiced meat. ...

'Come on Tim!' Boz was beckoning in the gloom. 'I've found us a seat.' He took his place opposite Boz who was already speaking to his neighbour in Welsh. He looked about him. They were sitting at a long table which ran to the full length of the low, windowless building. White candles had been set into saucers for sconces, their soft glow lighting up the faces of the customers who sat on benches either side. Some were in conversation – heads close together; some were laughing out loud; others were silent, jabbing at their loaded plates and forking gobbets of food into their waiting mouths. He felt that he was an unwilling part of a Bruegel painting; that he did not belong in this convivial penumbra where everybody knew everyone else …

'You're a long way away, Tim.' Boz had finished his conversation and was grinning at him over the candle light. Tim was aware that other eyes were upon him.

'We've got to order our food,' Boz continued; 'we're on at two.'

'Do they have a menu?' Tim's question was greeted with ribald laughter.

Boz came to the rescue. 'Give him a chance boys! No need for a menu, Tim. There's only one dish.'

'What's that?'

'Faggots and peas. The faggots are made in heaven …'

'And I doubt that the gentleman has had peas like these before.' The man next to Boz had interrupted in studied English and was pointing at a green slime on his plate. Boz signalled to a plump, apron clad woman standing in a doorway at the far end of the building. She vanished into a mist and re-emerged with two loaded plates and two mugs of milky tea. Boz and the woman, her brown hair done up in a bun, her dark eyes gleaming in the candle light, were sharing a joke or so it seemed for they spoke, as everyone here did, in Welsh. Boz pressed coins into her hand. She threw back her head and laughed; beamed at Tim and returned to her kitchen.

Tim was scouring his pockets for change. 'I must pay … at least for my share.'

'On me this time,' said Boz, waving him away. 'Next time you can pay.'

Tim was wondering whether he could stomach a next time. He studied the dish in front of him. In the dim light the green purulence of what must once have been peas looked repellent and concealed what looked like two large meatballs. … These had, by common consent, been among the most dreaded of the cooks' creations at school – composed, mostly, of large lumps of gristle which had to be chewed and chewed before being spat out into a handkerchief and concealed in a pocket ready for the fat house cat. The goodie-goodies and those luckless souls who sat next to masters would swallow the sickening lumps as best they could without throwing up. …

'Eat up Tim,' said Boz, already half way through his food. Cutlery was stowed upright in jars upon the table and sugar in open bowls, the spoons caked with the product of many stirrings. Tim added a spoonful to his mug and sipped the warm, sweet tea. It revived him. He looked down at the meatballs again. There was no way out. In this company he would have to eat the lot. He reached for a fork and plunged it into the meat releasing a steam smelling of hot onion and spice.

Boz watched him finish. 'I think you needed that … after your session with the Brigadier.'

'Did you hear what happened?'

'Another cock-up was there?'

'Yes, but it was my fault. I got the colours mixed up.'

'I doubt it was all your fault. He goes too fast. ... It's as if he can't wait to get it over with.'

'Why does he do it, then?'

'Search me. He doesn't have to. He's a qualified land agent; took his exams late in life – after the war and, in fairness, he's damned good at dealing with tenants' complaints and disputes. He won't have any nonsense; cuts them dead when they're creating and they respect him because they know where he's been.' ... Boz paused. 'Did you know what he did in the army?'

'No.'... Tim was aware that Boz and he had become the focus of attention by the men on both sides of them.

'Well,' Boz continued, 'between the wars he spent a lot of time on the North-West Frontier – trying to keep the Afghans in order; dangerous stuff. He had a desk in the last war; too old for combat. In fairness, knowing him, I think he'd have preferred to have been in the thick of it.'...

The man sitting to the right of Tim nudged him. 'If the Brigadier can call himself "Brigadier," then this man,' he nodded towards Boz, 'should be called "Captain."'

. 'He's entitled. He's been a professional,' Boz countered; 'and, by the way, Tim, we don't call him "The Brigadier" round here. He's "The Brig" for short.'

The man next to Tim was not to be put off. 'You are talking with a brave man and...'

Boz cut in; 'Peid, John; ... dim rhagor.'

Tim knew few Welsh words but no dictionary was needed to establish that Boz did not want the conversation to continue. His modesty regarding matters of such apparent importance seemed admirable. ...

'Fair play to the Brig,' continued Boz, breaking the silence which had followed his admonition; 'I don't think that the pig prices suffer. The bidders see to that and I think a lot of the men go there every week for the entertainment. Something always seems to go wrong and then they go and have a laugh about it in "The Cow."'

At four o'clock Tim was walking towards the hut. The selling with Boz had been an encouraging experience; no mistakes thanks, largely, to his knowledge of his customers. He sold like a poet – a rhythmic flow of words rolling effortlessly off the tongue and spiked with an instant wit, born of circumstance. The crowd had been good-humoured throughout and the cattle all sold. Tim was feeling pleased with himself as he pushed open the door. The place was silent. The Brig, who was leaning over the counter in conversation with one of the girls, straightened up, turned and glared at him. 'I've got a bone to pick with you, Barrington-Lewis! Will you attempt to translate these?' He handed Tim three sale sheets and sighed – 'if I didn't know any better I would have concluded that you were a very incompetent scribe for one of the Pharaohs.'

Tim studied his handwriting in dismay, his mind a blank. 'It was when I got behind, sir; my hand wouldn't work.'

'Wouldn't work?'

'I'll do what I can, sir.'

'I should bloody well hope so or we won't know where the hell we are. I thought you'd been to a good school!' The Brig looked at his watch and made for the door. 'I'll be back in about ten minutes. Hopefully you'll have made some sense of it by then.' The door slammed shut and the girls, who had witnessed his dressing down, started talking to each other – in Welsh.

'Don't worry,' said Eleri, taking the sheets from him; 'all the other pages were right and you've got all the prices and colours on these. It's just half a dozen names and addresses we can't read. Can you remember what the buyers looked like?'

'They all looked the same to me.'

'Well; Rhian and I are going to check through the regular buyers; we may be able to work it out from ...' Eleri stopped in mid sentence, peering out of the window. 'Duw! ...That's lucky. I thought he'd be in the pub by now.' She lifted the counter-hatch and ran outside. Half a minute later she was back with the hunch-backed runner. He carefully studied the offending sale-sheets and, after what seemed minimal consideration, quietly recited names and addresses. He looked up at Tim and smiled. 'All done; I know them all; ... and I found that first buyer.'

'I seem to have been a bit of a nuisance.'

'Not at all. Very understandable in the circumstances.'

Tim paused outside the hut and sighed. He would like to have said more to the runner. The elderly man's detailed knowledge of those who lived in this agricultural community was something that could never be learned in a college or university – a country wisdom unknown to those who had gone to so-called "good" schools.

Boz was walking towards him. 'Come on, Tim. We're going for a drink.'...

The "Contented Cow", its green-painted doors flung wide

to welcome both those who had made some money on the day and those who were nursing their losses, enjoyed a prime position opposite the market entrance. Inside, a gathering of boisterous men, some large, some small, laughing and shouting, stood in a haze of smoke. Tim looked about him. The ceiling had turned a nicotine brown and the floor was of grimy boards. Two harassed-looking, blonde girls toiled behind a counter. He must have been the only customer in shoes; all others wore boots but the dull, grey uniform of dustcoats and caps had been laid aside – revealing individual faces and characters; some bald, some hairy, in old jackets, patched twill or corduroy trousers and colourful pullovers. The language was universally Welsh. Boz returned from the bar and handed him a whisky.

'That's large,' exclaimed Tim, holding his glass to the light.

Boz laughed. 'It's a double; what else? … I've added some water for you.' Tim reached into his pocket for the packet of ten cigarettes. There were three left. He offered one to Boz who waved it away, tapping his glass. 'This is my poison.'

'I only smoke when I'm drinking.'

'That's what they all say.'

'Honestly; … my mother won't let me smoke in the house.'

'And your father?'

Tim lit his cigarette, drew deep and exhaled. 'He's dead; … killed near the end of the war.'

Boz stalled, his features changed to an instant solemnity. He reached out and patted Tim on the shoulder. 'I shouldn't have asked that, should I?'

'It doesn't matter. How could you have known?'

'Well I know now; ... and if you get any problems with anyone here you come to me; ...and there are a few things you need to know. Firstly – the job's not all this. You'll probably be in the market on Mondays only and I'll do my best to get you into the cattle ring. That's a bloody sight easier than the pigs – all things considered. Secondly, you really need to learn some Welsh; otherwise you'll only know half of what's going on – like the Brig...' An enormous, balding man with wild eyes had come out of the crowd and grabbed Boz's glass. 'Un bach to, Boz.' The giant's voice was paradoxically small and squeaky.

'Dim ond un, Sam,' Boz replied.

The giant looked Tim up and down. 'Pwy iw e?' Boz quickly replied in Welsh and the man disappeared to the bar. Tim had spotted the runner, perched on one of the few bar stools and hunched over the end of the counter.

'That's Dai,' said Boz, following his gaze; 'one of the best; but he's had bad luck in his time.'

Tim was interested to know more of his unlikely saviour and for whom he now had a name. 'What sort of bad luck?'

'He owned a farm once – up in the hills near Twll; a good one but he over-extended himself with the bloody bank and the receiver got the lot! ... Then, as if that wasn't enough, his back started to bend. .... He and his wife have ended up living in a small terrace house in town and now he works for us to make ends meet, the poor bugger.'

'I owe him a drink,' said Tim.

'Good idea. ... They say he drinks to kill the pain.' Boz paused ... 'Why don't you join him now? Big Sam's got my glass and I'll have to stop him putting half a bottle in it.' Tim looked towards the bar where the giant stood – waving a tumbler of liquor. ...

The runner was looking down at a glass which was empty. At first Tim wondered whether he wanted to be left alone. 'Can I get you another?' he whispered.

The man raised his head. 'I did not expect to see you here, Mr ...'

'Please call me Tim.'

'Your Christian name; I could not call you that. It would not be fitting.'

'Can I get you another whisky?'

'That is very kind of you.'

Tim bought him a double and added a single to his own. The ten shilling note in his wallet was the last and only half came back by way of change. The man reached across the counter, grasped a jug, added water and raised his tumbler, his rigid posture allowing him only to sip the spirit off the top of the glass.

'Thank you for your help with the pigs,' said Tim, aware that upturned, dark and kindly eyes were studying him closely. 'If it wasn't for you, I'd still be trying to work things out.'

The man's face creased into a smile. 'Will it be proper if I call you "Mr Tim?"'

Light was fading as Tim left "The Contented Cow." He went up a winding street of small, terraced houses; then through a narrow cut between taller buildings. Alcohol had expunged the embarrassments of the day and lightened his step as he headed down the High Street. He looked about him. The place seemed strangely deserted for a market day. People in two's and three's were gathered in shop doorways but few were looking at the merchandise. They seemed to be looking at him. He quickened his pace – passing a bank, the Post Office and a bakery. He paused at London House, its curving, plate glass windows displaying rolls of fabric and hats Mother wouldn't be seen dead in.

'I would come in here if I were you.' A stunted, wiry man in a brown dustcoat and smoking a drooping roll-up was beckoning from the doorway.

'I don't want to buy anything,' Tim muttered, beginning to walk on but the man reached out, grabbed him by the arm and drew him into the space between the shop windows. 'You're with the auctioneers, aren't you?' he asked, his breath stinking of stale beer and tobacco.

'Yes,' said Tim, defensively

'Well, you should know better,' said the man, loosening his grip.

'Better about what?'

'The beef cattle sold in the market; every Monday they catch the five o'clock train so they've got to get to the station somehow.'

'What's that got to do with me?' asked Tim, beginning to doubt the sanity of his unwanted companion.

'You'll soon find out. … They drive them through the town, see.'

'What! The High Street?'

'It's the shortest distance. With drovers at the junctions the buggers don't often stray.' … The man cocked an ear. … 'Can you hear them?' Without waiting for an answer he took up his stick and moved forward to the edge of the pavement, dropping his roll-up and grinding it out with his foot. He looked back at Tim. 'Now you stand behind me; and don't move.'

Tim could hear the cries of drovers and the distant thundering of hooves. He looked to the left. A shimmering at the far end of the street was resolving into a herd of black, roan, red and white cattle, some with horns, some without, charging towards him. As the stampede went past the man cried out and waved his stick at them. When they had gone he turned back and winked at Tim 'You glad I pulled you in? … If you'd stayed out in the street they'd have taken you to the station by now.'

'Can't they take them in lorries?'

'You don't know much, do you,' said the man, spitting in the gutter, rolling another cigarette. 'Those cattle were bought by dealers to order or for selling on – in England, mostly. Those English buggers like their Welsh beef. The dealers have got to turn a profit, see; and trains is cheapest to take that many.'

'Don't people object to them coming through the town?'

'It doesn't bother them; been going on for as long as anyone can remember and before that, no doubt.'

'Has anyone been hurt?',

'No one I know; other than you might have been – just now. People here know when they're coming, see; … but, to tell the truth, there have been a few commotions. About two years ago we had one wild bullock; a big beast he was; charged straight through the window behind you; came to a stop at the counter, grunting and pawing the ground, they say; gave the staff a hell of a fright, I can tell you; but there was a funny side. The bullock had a woman's hat on one of its horns – skewered right through.'... The man paused, his laughter coarse and wheezing. ... 'That's why I'm standing here every week. Fair play, they don't want another beast in there, do they? ... We don't often see bullocks like that; ... not properly cut, you see.'

'Cut?'

'Half a bull,' sighed the man, turning to go; 'you have a lot to learn, you poor bugger. ... Now mind you don't tread in any shit.'

# CHAPTER 2

Tegwyn Bartholomeus Lewis stood in front of the long mirror on his wardrobe door. He felt content. Breakfast had been made and he would be early as usual. He tightened his black tie, adjusted his braces and patted the shoulders of his sombre pinstripe; then reached for his bowler, perched on the bedside table. The thing would insist on sliding over his temples, coming to rest on the tips of his ears and bending them over a little. 'London House' had happily allowed him to borrow a smaller size for a day at no cost but the rim had mercilessly squeezed his brow and given him a headache. It had been returned with thanks. ... Tegwyn checked the smoothness of his chin; then leaned forward to the mirror and neatly plucked a hair protruding from his nose. Tidiness was remarkably close to godliness in these parts and he had a reputation to keep. Armed with no paper qualifications whatsoever in the mysteries of auctioneering he had, over the years, become the undisputed master of the art of clerking. His knowledge of buyers and sellers, where they lived, who they lived with and what they were up to was legendary. This gift extended to all but the latest arrivals in Rhywle and Twll but even those would be gathered into his encyclopaedic memory in time. For him his ability stemmed from an enduring interest in people to the exclusion of almost everything else and which the minister of Bethesda had once kindly suggested was born of unselfishness. Yes – he could live with that on his tombstone alright but there was another gift which flowed from it; one which had made him a vital cog in the wheel of the firm and had provided him with a room of his own, albeit a small one and a car which matched the necessity of his duties. ... He was universally regarded as unequalled in the art of obsequy. Four pennies crashing to the bottom of a coin box, followed by heavy breathing, followed by the confirmation of a sad passing in the rural fastnesses would send him scurrying to the Riley fifteen-hundred saloon waiting in the office car park reserved for him and the partners. It was vital to be first at a death and important to know what to say when one got there. He would speed through country lanes he had known from his childhood whilst dwelling upon what virtues could be assembled for the departed. This meant that, upon arrival, he could deliver his condolences extempore; his soft voice, sallow features and damp, brown eyes radiating the required gravitas. He may have been short in stature but he stood straight in his neat suit and his bowler, presenting an appropriate combination of respect and modesty. He was particularly accomplished with widows. There was something indefinable which drew them to him although there had been no women in his life beyond Mother. ... Tegwyn sighed; then smiled. His latest triumph had been last week – securing instructions to sell a two hundred and fifty acre farm and all of its live and dead stock. The funeral, in Jabez Chapel, was this afternoon and it was essential that he be there. Tegwyn sighed again. ... Ministers in double figures were reputed to be queuing up to speak of the dead. It would be a long job; that was for sure and his attendance at the food-burdened, spirit-laden wake was equally essential. Slip up now and those cocky upstarts, who had opened in opposition across the square, could still get it. They had set up two years ago with marble pillars, of all things, either side of a massive, oak-panelled front door. These pale imitations of ancient Rome had served to impress the citizens of Rhywle and Twll and the wild countryside in between. Many clients had been lost – leading to a hurried patching and redecoration of the office front. Worse still, the opposition had invested in a car which was even faster than his and he had, on a number of occasions, suffered the dreadful humiliation of being beaten in the race to a body; ... but things had changed. The widows, in particular, had compared notes as to the content and eloquence of the condolences offered and had discovered that the other lot were working off some kind of pre-ordained lament, whereas his offerings were fresh off the tongue with detailed knowledge of the dead every time. Wayward clients had come flowing back in – a tide which had carried him to an improved status in the firm. ... Mother would have been proud. ... He removed his bowler and reached for a comb. There was not much left of his hair, chestnut turning to silver but, at least, it looked fitting for a man of his age. When he had finished he replaced the hat, wiped off his shoulders and headed downstairs to his neat kitchen where the teapot waited under its cosy and the boiled egg stood in its cup.

Tegwyn arrived at the office on the stroke of half past eight, doffed his hat to the girls taking off their coats and gossiping in reception and headed for his room. This was his special place; the centre of his world as a man of affairs. Here private concerns could be forgotten in the pursuit of his duties. The room was large enough for a small desk with a chair either side of it and a bookcase furnished with volumes of Welsh poetry, historic registers of famous beasts, a copy of the Auctioneers' Bidding Agreements Act 1927 prominently displayed, back copies of the Farmers Weekly and a large Bible. The one window overlooked a blank wall of decaying brickwork – but no matter. He would not wish for the view of the river enjoyed by the partners on the first floor. It would be a distraction. Besides, he had his two pictures to gaze upon; the one – a prize-winning ram and the other – a bull of prodigious proportions, set against a rural background which reminded him of the gentle hills and bosky woods he could observe from his parlour window.

Upon the desk stood a fat, black telephone with many buttons connecting him to reception and the outside world and, to one side, a wooden tray with a pile of neat, cardboard files. He picked one up and opened it. This morning he would check the Monday market records to ensure that all names and addresses on invoices were present and correct. This afternoon it was the funeral. ... The phone rang and he picked up the receiver. ... It was Rhian.

'Your special order is in, Mr Lewis.'

'What order?'

'I don't know.'

'Is it here?'

'No, it's with the chemist.'

'Thank you.' Tegwyn put the receiver down thoughtfully. A cloud had obscured his horizon. What, in the name of all that was holy, had he ordered from the chemist? He knew many who had joined the ranks of the forgetful but surely not himself – at least not yet. When had he last been there? … Friday, of course, but not in the shop. … Glyn Jenkins, the one chemist in Rhywle, enjoyed the kind of respect that only a professional man in a small town could aspire to – this in spite of the fact that he also held a licence to sell alcohol in a small but comfortable room to the rear of his premises. This conjunction of occupations had not troubled the citizens of Rhywle, most of whom, not without good reason, regarded alcohol as a substance which, modestly consumed, would, more often than not, make you feel better than any potion the doctors could come up with. In that it would not have been fitting for such a facility to be open to the public at large it had, from the start, been restricted, by invitation, to the elite of the town who met regularly on Tuesdays and Fridays from the issuance of the last prescription to closing time which, according to the quality of the company and conversation, was a moveable affair. … The call had come two years ago and Tegwyn had willingly responded for to be a member of an assembly which included two solicitors, two doctors, an accountant, a surveyor and, of course, Glyn himself was an honour indeed. Besides which the place was a hive of gossip and speculation and much could be gleaned there. There had been one reservation. Having in his youth flirted with "The Band of Hope" he drank next to nothing but even that defect had turned to advantage – for his moderation had been taken as gravitas by his inebriated companions. … Tegwyn put his hand to his brow. … On Friday he had been particularly abstemious, consuming a mere half pint of shandy before returning home to prepare for the Saturday meeting of The Twll

Agricultural Show committee; his first as president elect. Surely he would remember if he had placed any kind of order with Glyn. ...

Glyn's premises enjoyed pride of place in the High Street. Tegwyn nervously pushed open the plate glass door in its swirling mahogany frame. He tipped his bowler to the two, white-coated girls behind the counter.

'Good morning ladies.'

'Good morning, Mr Lewis.' The reply came as a cheeky chorus and the girls seemed to be smirking.

'Could I speak with Mr Jenkins?'

One of the girls disappeared into the dispensary while the other rearranged cosmetics which Tegwyn thought could just as well be left as they were.

'Teg ... a word.' Glyn, wearing his white coat of office, was gesturing him to the insubstantial alcove at the far end of the counter; a confessional where customers could whisper their more embarrassing bodily afflictions in the hope of relief. Glyn, whose rounded, urbane countenance normally radiated a comforting certainty, was looking puzzled. He was holding a parcel wrapped in brown paper.

'I got a message in the office,' Tegwyn muttered, ... 'about a special delivery for me.'

Glyn ran his pink fingers through the remains of his silken hair, adjusted gold-rimmed lunettes upon his large, red nose and observed Tegwyn. 'This is it, Teg; ... but I must explain. They came in loose; in separate boxes; so we packed them up for you. It seemed more fitting in the circumstances.' Tegwyn could hear stifled laughter beyond the flimsy partition which shielded him from the outside world and felt uneasy. Glyn raised his head and shouted. 'Get on with your work girls.'

Tegwyn leaned forward and whispered. 'What's in the boxes?'

'Don't you know?'

'I don't remember ordering anything.'

Glyn winked at him. 'Come on, Teg; nothing to be ashamed of. We're all men of the world.' Glyn produced a piece of note-paper. 'Look ... we got your order in writing and signed.'

Tegwyn peered at it. 'But it is typewritten. Is that my signature?'

'Looks like it to me; and there's nothing to pay.'

'You got the money?'

'In cash; paid in advance with the order; posted through the door in a brown envelope addressed to me personally; very professional and considerate to the ladies if I might say. Anyway Teg here they are – ready to take away and nothing said; and very sensible to order in bulk. Good economy; typical of you.' Tegwyn, who could feel blood pounding in his cheeks for a reason he did not know, was lost for words. Glyn grinned at him and whispered. 'You're a dark horse, Teg. Who's the lucky lady?'...

Tegwyn locked the door of his office and placed the parcel on his desk. He examined it; then shook it. There was no rattling. He hurriedly removed the brown paper and found a cardboard box tied with a piece of string. He reached for the scissors, cut the string, opened the box and looked inside.

There were a number of smaller boxes, neatly wrapped in cellophane. He removed one, put on his glasses and studied the small print commencing 'Instructions for use.'

Tim had survived his first few weeks and had found refuge in the estates maintenance and drawing office on the second floor. This was a place of relative calm to which he had been assigned between worrying bouts of clerking in the market and a few farm visits with partners. His duties here were not arduous – largely concerned with tracing the field boundaries of farms from Ordnance Survey maps kept in separate drawers and, more often than not, out of order. His desk was a sloping wooden structure at which he could stand or sit on a high stool. The tracings were executed on translucent, blue linen which had a pleasant, leathery smell and felt good to the touch. He had quickly mastered the art of cutting the precious material from its roll, using the open jaws of a sharp scissors in one swift and confident movement leaving a clean, straight edge. He was pleased that his efforts would be sown into title deeds and would thus be of a permanent nature. Jim, who had no recognisable qualifications other than experience, ran this quiet corner of the practice with gentle good humour. A modest man, brought up in the Welsh language, he had become the undisputed master of the art of procrastination when dealing with tenants – apparently yielding to ambitious demands for improvement; then gently wearing them down over time – ultimately reducing the cost to the size of the landlord's purse without rancour on either side. ...

Tim was looking out of the window in front of his desk.

The pitiful remains of Rhywle Castle were heaped upon a mound to the far side of the river. The sun was casting long shadows among its moss-covered stones and lighting up the meadows beyond where cattle were grazing. ... He fixed the map to his desk top; then the linen. He took up his mapping pen. The trick was to get a drop of ink to lodge between the two blades of the pen which could then be manipulated, by means of an adjusting screw, to provide clean lines of different thicknesses. Get it wrong and there was a hell of a mess which, when dry, might be scraped off with a razor blade if you were lucky. If not, the linen was lost. Tim offered up his straight edge and drew the first line. ... There was a tap on his shoulder. He turned to face Boz.

'Tim; ... can you do me a real favour?'

'If I can; ...what is it?

'Well, it's a bit complicated.'

'How complicated?'

'It seems that persons unknown have clubbed together to buy a load of French letters and have had them delivered to Tegwyn.'

'Oh!'... Tim's knowledge of French letters was limited to the incident at school when Rhyd had acquired a dozen of the things and persuaded James and himself to raid the school chaplain's garden under cover of darkness. There they had filled them with water from the hose and hung them in the shrubbery. In the moonlight they had looked remarkably lewd. In the event it was deeply unfortunate that they had remained undiscovered until the following evening when some of the chaplain's cocktail-party guests had decided to explore. The ensuing gossip had run the length and breadth of the school and beyond. Exeats and other privileges for the entire school had been withdrawn pending identification of the culprits. Conscience had got the better of him and he had persuaded Rhyd and James to join him in owning up. The consequences had been dire. They had nearly been expelled, saved only by a savage beating at the hands of the headmaster; followed by grovelling letters of apology to the chaplain's wife. He had, at the last minute, decided to send flowers with his letter which had drawn a reply from the lady suggesting that all hope of his becoming a gentleman had not been lost. ...

'What do you want me to do?'

'It's quite funny when you think of it; but Teg's so embarrassed that he's locked himself in his room and won't come out; and he's due at a funeral this afternoon. If he doesn't make that there'll be hell to pay. ... Can you speak with him?'

'Why me?'

'I've had nothing to do with it but, take it from me, the rest of us are under suspicion. You're so new here that you can't possibly have been part of the stupid prank. He just needs a shoulder to cry on if you know what I mean.' ...

Tim stopped outside Tegwyn's door. What the hell was he doing? He knew little of Tegwyn other than exchanges of pleasantries. He took a deep breath and tapped.

'Who is it?' The voice sounded weak.

'It's Tim Barrington-Lewis.'

There was a pause; then a movement. The key turned in the lock and the door opened a quarter. Tegwyn's mournful face appeared in the gap. 'You can come in,' said Tegwyn pointedly, gesturing Tim to a chair. ...'What can I do for you,

Mr Tim?'

'I ... I came about the parcel.'

'Is it yours?' asked Tegwyn, hopefully.

'No, it isn't.'

'Surely you didn't order it for me, Mr Tim?'

'No; ... absolutely not; but someone told me you were ... so I thought ... you might like ....' Tim was blushing in the knowledge that he was making a mess of things. Eyes, red as a mourner's, scanned him up and down. ... 'You have a kind face, Mr Tim,' Tegwyn sighed, 'and I am in need of kindness at the moment.'

'It sounds as though it was some kind of practical joke,' said Tim, believing he had found an opening; 'and, may'be, no one in the office was involved.'

'Some joke!' Tegwyn reached to the floor and brought up a cardboard box. In a gesture of annoyance he turned it upside down and shook its contents onto the desk to form an untidy ziggurat of smaller boxes.

'How many are there?' asked Tim, anxious to keep the conversation going.

'Twenty boxes,' cried Tegwyn, burying his head in his hands and clutching at the remains of his hair, 'and it says there are five of the dreadful things in each. ...That makes a hundred. ... I'm ruined!'

Tim, recognising that he had asked the wrong question, decided to blot it out with another. 'Could anyone really want so many of them at one time?'

'Quite so,' Tegwyn groaned. ... 'It will be all over the office already and, by tonight, it will be all over town. Tomorrow it will get to Twll. ... They'll think I'm some kind of a maniac! I won't be able to go anywhere. ... They'll throw me out of the club. ... The women and, probably, most of the men will not think it fitting for me to attend funerals! ... My poor mother will be turning in her grave! ... My God,' wailed Tegwyn, breathing heavily, 'and there's worse! They surely won't let me remain an Elder of Bethesda.'

'That would be very unforgiving.'

'They're not a very forgiving lot.'

'The truth is you didn't order those ... things,' said Tim, knowing that to avoid a descent into utter despair he had, somehow, to change tack. 'Others did and it doesn't matter who they are really.'

'Oh yes it does,' Tegwyn cried, his face flushing with anger, his thin voice raised. 'They've brought me to this shame. I shall lose all respect ... and there's another thing. I have recently been given the honour of becoming president elect of the Twll Agricultural Society. I shall have to resign in disgrace before even taking office!'

'It's quite legal to buy these things and it doesn't matter how many really,' countered Tim.

Tegwyn looked thoughtful; then straightened up. 'I have been sitting here for most of the morning trying to find a solution and there is only one that might help.'

'What's that?' asked Tim, hopefully.

'I must immediately place an announcement in the Twll Trumpet denying all knowledge.'

'I wouldn't do that.'

'Why not?'

'You'll bring it to everybody's attention and they might think there's no smoke without a fire.'

'Oh,' Tegwyn howled, 'and there are so many in Twll who would prefer it to be a fire! Nothing much happens there and this will be like manna from heaven to them.'

In the wake of this outburst and the dismal silence which had settled upon them both, the blank in Tim's mind began to be filled with an inspiration of remarkable simplicity. It seemed worth a try. 'Your name is Tegwyn Lewis?'

Tegwyn was looking puzzled. 'Yes, Mr Tim.'

'But what's your full name? I remember seeing a letter in reception addressed to you with a "B" in it.'

'Tegwyn Bartholomeus Lewis if you want to know, Mr Tim. ... It's a big name for a small man I'm ashamed to say.'

'What if I were to say that I had ordered those things for myself?'

'But the order had my name on it – "T.B. Lewis" and this office as my address. I saw it with my own eyes!'

'Yes; but what is my name?'

'Mr Tim ... Barrington-Lewis.' Tegwyn's features registered that he had grasped a significance.

'And I don't always use the Barrington bit when I sign things. It could just as easily be "T.B-Lewis." ... I could tell the shop there's been a misunderstanding – you being asked to collect and not me.'

'But there's the signature; it looked very like mine on the order.'

'Whoever sent the order must have copied yours,' said Tim, feeling that he had regained the initiative. 'I could explain that our signatures are very similar. Has the bill been paid?'

'Yes; cash paid in advance would you believe.'

'Then the shop won't ask any questions.'

'I'm not so sure, Mr Tim. Glyn the chemist is a curious man. He may like to think I am consorting with ladies of the night though, God be thanked, I know of none around here. … People will believe that I'm a monster with the women!'

'I don't think they will,' said Tim, recognizing that nothing looked further from the truth.

'I will just have to pack up and leave,' sighed Tegwyn, wringing his neat hands until the knuckles were white.

'I'll go now and tell the people in the shop,' said Tim, reaching a decision.

'But you'd be telling a lie, Mr Tim,' said Tegwyn, sitting up and looking hopeful.

'In a good cause. Leave it to me.'

Tegwyn leaned forward. 'Why are you doing this for me?'

This was a question for which Tim was unprepared. 'Well,' he stumbled, 'you're obviously very upset about it.'

'And you are clearly a young gentleman from a respectable family, Mr Tim. Your reputation could be seriously damaged.'

Tim grinned nervously. 'It won't; … not unless my mother finds out.'

# CHAPTER 3

Tim's journey home had been an opportunity to reflect upon his day's work. His visit to the chemist's hadn't gone too badly. He had hovered outside the shop until there were no customers and had initially approached one of the girls behind the counter, feeling it might be less embarrassing if he simply left a message. He had hardly opened his mouth when the chemist had come out of his dispensary and shepherded him to a booth at the end of the counter. Tim had gabbled his lie regarding the confusion of names, feeling his face to be on fire and the silence which followed had been awful. He had glanced up at a kindly, bespectacled face which wore an expression lodged somewhere between amusement and disbelief but he had sensed a growing respect for his dissembling. The wonder of it was that the man knew his name already, including the Barrington bit and a lot more besides. … Truly this was a town with no secrets. This latest would soon be public knowledge but would it do him any harm? He was a long way from home and, may'be, he would now be taken as a man of the world and not an overgrown schoolboy. Tim smiled at the thought as he turned left into the narrow lane leading to the farm. The girls in the shop had been eyeing him up and down as he left and it was clear what they were thinking. …

Tim parked the Minor in the usual place under the tree and

sat, for a moment, considering what to do with the parcel in the boot. Stowing it at home was not an option. Mother might discover it with unimaginable consequences. Neither could he hide it in his bedroom here. Beth might find it and Mam might consider her house to have been defiled. He concluded that it would have to remain locked in the neutral territory of the boot for the time being but, even there, it could be discovered. He had already decided to keep a small supply for himself, just in case. The rest he would have to think about. ...

Mam was at the stove when Tim entered. She swung round holding a pan. 'Tim ...'Tac' is back!' She turned to a lanky figure sprawled untidily on the high backed settle, his feet extended towards the fire and frowned; 'and a week earlier than he should be. God knows what Lowri thinks of it!'

The old man peered at them and grinned mischievously. 'We're speaking English now, are we? ... Lowri and the boys are all one could hope for but London for a month is a bugger.'

'Tac doesn't mean to be rude,' said Mam, apologetically.

'Don't make excuses for me, Mari!' shouted the old man, standing up with the aid of a stick, his back to the fire. His dark eyes, set deep in a wrinkled face and enlarged by heavy lenses in thick, black, circular frames, were fixed on Tim. 'He looks like a gentleman. ... I am sure we will get on. What is his name again?'

'He's got a memory like a sieve,' Mam muttered. 'I don't know how many times I've told him.'

The old man was still looking at Tim. 'What did she say?'

'Why aren't you wearing your deaf aid?' shouted Mam.

'Tim, sir; my name is Tim,' said Tim, raising his voice; wanting to stop the row.

'No need for the "sir" boy. You only make me feel older than I am and that is bad enough. ... Where do you come from?'

'Pembrokeshire; near St Davids.'

'The holy city; but there are a lot of English down there.'

'We used to live in Herefordshire.'

'A border man; ... why did you move?'

'It's no business of yours,' snapped Mam, wagging her finger.

'My mother had friends in the area,' said Tim, hoping not to be drawn into further explanation.

The old man picked up a poker and started prodding the fire. 'Come and sit on the sgiw, Tim. There's time before supper. Mari will bring us some tea.'

The sgiw was surprisingly comfortable, its high back excluding draughts and enfolding its occupants in the private world of the fireplace. A few minutes later Mam brought him a mug of hot, sweet tea, whitened with farm milk. It had taken some time to wean her off the idea that a cup and saucer were the only appropriate vessels for him. 'You'll have to forgive him,' she whispered; 'he's always so full of questions.' His elderly neighbour was concentrating upon the filling of his pipe. He had stopped half way to take a noisy sip of his dark tea and had then continued with the ritual. Tim was aching to speak but what could he say to a complete stranger who seemed unpredictable and who would, no doubt, have preferred to speak in Welsh. When the pipe was ignited the old man sucked on its smoke, coughed noisily, spat into the fire and croaked 'thank God I am home. Lowri would never let me do this in her house. She says the place would stink for days and that it is bad for me.'...

'She's right,' cried Mam from the stove; 'she's not a nurse for nothing.'

'And bossy with it,' retorted the old man. 'Why should I stop at my age? ... Here, at least, the whole lot goes up the chimney; so much for their central heating!' The old man put his pipe on the hearth, stood up slowly, opened a small cupboard above the chimney arch, produced a bottle of whisky and pulled out its cork. 'This is what you need after a day's work,' he said, pouring a large measure into Tim's mug.

'Don't let him lead you astray,' cried Mam; 'he has many bad habits.'

Tim sipped at the tea. The combination of the sharpness of leaf, the spicy warmth and potency of the spirit was a revelation. The old man stooped over him and sniffed noisily at the fumes. 'Well ... What do you think?'

'It's good; really good, thank you'

The old man picked up his pipe again and started to relight it. 'It is what we call Welsh tea; just what a farmer wants after a day in the cold.' ...

Geraint and Beth came in late from the milking. Over supper there was an irritable exchange in Welsh between Geraint and the old man which had left Tim feeling awkward. The old man winked at him and said 'They were herding them in when Gwenllian bolted for it. She had covered three muddy fields by the time they caught up with her and ...

'I think Tim needs to know who Gwenllian is,' said Mam.

The old man laughed. 'She might as well be a woman the way she behaves. She is a cow ... and a bugger besides.'

'He really does shame me sometimes,' said Mam, raising her voice; 'and at the table too.' The old man had a wicked look in his eye but the silence which followed was, surprisingly, broken by Geraint's deep and solemn voice. 'Whatever anyone says she is probably one of the best Dams in the herd. Her yields are good and she will suckle a calf like no other.' Tim looked up from his plate of ham, potatoes and pickled beetroot. It was the first time that this taciturn giant of a young Welshman, whose dark and brooding eyes were now fixed upon him, had spoken to him directly. It seemed that Geraint rarely spoke in English but, when he did, his voice had the manly clarity and formality of an actor who had learned his lines well.

Tim, who had felt irrelevant and intimidated in his company, was searching for a reply which would please him and, may'be, open up a line of communication. 'How many cattle do you have in the herd?'

The big man's eyes shone. 'Forty-seven milkers,' he answered thoughtfully; 'all pedigree Friesian. Then there are the followers, sucklers and calves. You have got to keep them coming, you see; a lifetime's work and it never stops. If it does you are finished.'...

After supper the old man insisted upon having further conversation with Tim who would have preferred an opportunity to read the letter which Mam had handed to him upon his return from work. This, in Rhyd's handwriting and with an

Oxford postmark, was roosting in his breast pocket.

The fire in front of them spat and crackled under its consignment of fresh logs. The pipe was being rekindled. In the silent space Tim was considering the problem of names and decided that 'Tac' was too familiar a term for his elderly neighbour. The old man drew on his pipe and turned to him. 'Do you speak any Welsh at all?'

'None, I'm afraid.'

'You will have to learn some where you are working or they will think you are twp; half-witted. Does anyone in your family speak it?'

'No; ... neither my mother nor my sister.'

'What about your father?'

Tim stalled. An aching dread was taking him over. There seemed no way out other than to clam up. 'He's dead. ... He died in the war.' Tim's bleak reply was more in the form of an exhalation than speech. The old man sat in silence for what seemed a long time. Then, without a word, he stood up with the aid of his stick and went into the scullery. Tim could hear a muffled conversation and Mam's long sigh. The old man returned with a clay jug of water and placed it on the sgiw; then he reached up to the cupboard. Tim was staring at the fire wondering what to say next. His answer had been so brief, uninformative, blunt even; but that is how the loss of his father had always felt. No one, not even Rhyd, had ever asked for the details which lay in a folder tied with a red ribbon in the top drawer of mother's bedside table. A glass was thrust into his hand. It was half full of whisky. The old man picked up the jug and filled the tumbler to the brim. 'You must add water to put out the fire,' he said; 'then it gains flavour; but not with any old water. This comes from the spring in our bluebell wood; straight out of the rock, sweet and clear. I built the cavam and laid the pipe myself but I was younger then.' The old man sat down with a groan. 'Do you want to tell me about it?'

Tim groped in his jacket pocket and found the crinkled packet of ten. 'Do you mind if I smoke one of these?'

'Me ... mind; with this,' said the old man, waving his pipe.

Tim opened the packet. There were six left. He lit one and inhaled deeply. He watched the smoke catch in the current of hot air and disappear up the waiting throat of the chimney. He raised his glass and drank. Now the old man was fiddling with his deaf aid, its squawks of discontent punctuated by his infuriated mutterings. ... His talent for inquisition had been unexpected. When Tim spoke his voice seemed not to belong; to be coming from some hushed, distant part of him like the waves of a reluctant sea. ...

'It was at the end of the war. ... His company was in Berlin ... trying to keep order on the streets. ... It was chaos – with starving children everywhere. ... My father and his men were sharing rations with them. ... A small boy was running across the street to where food was being handed out. ... They say he didn't see the lorry but my father did and rushed into the road to push him out of the way; ... but it was too late ... for my father.' Tim drew on his cigarette and swallowed more whisky.

The old man's reply was a long time coming. 'Was the child saved?'

'Yes.'

'Then your father did a brave and selfless thing.'

45

'Yes, but to fight his way across Europe, be promoted on the field and end up being run over by a British army lorry after the war had ended.' Tim could feel his eyes moistening and rubbed at them. He knew that the alcohol was lowering his defences but he didn't care any more. 'His commanding officer wrote to my mother saying that he ought to have had a medal for what he did. .... His sergeant wrote and a lot of the men did as well. ... My mother has all the letters. ... The trouble is ... I can't really remember what he looked or sounded like. All that's left are a few photographs. ... I was about the same age as the child he saved.'

A heavy silence settled between them before the questioning continued. 'Has your mother ever heard from the boy?'

'Nothing, until last Christmas. ... He'd traced us through military records. His letter was forwarded by the War Office.'

'It must have been good for your mother to receive that letter.'

'I suppose it was; but it brought it all back to her.' The memory of Mother quietly weeping behind the locked door of her bedroom was still clear.

'What is he doing with the life your father gave him?'

Tim brightened. The suggestion that the death of his father was inextricably bound up with a new life among former enemies had been something he'd never considered; an idea which seemed, at once, paradoxical and attractive. 'Friedrich ... he's doing physics and maths at University. ... It seems he's very intelligent; clever enough to trace my mother anyway.'

'In his time he may discover something that changes the

world for the better, Tim. Have you ever thought of that?'

'Not really.'

'Then you should. That way your father's death will be easier to bear. It will seem part of a scheme of things. ... Do you want to meet the lad?'

'I haven't really thought about it. Mother did reply to his letter and he wrote back. ... He may visit us next summer.'

'Do you have a brother, Tim?'

'No.'

'Then this German lad could be like a brother to you. Your father was responsible for both of you if you think about it. ...Write to him. Send him a photograph.'

'I suppose I should.'

The old man leaned forward and tapped out his pipe on the hearthstone. 'There must be times when you feel lonely, Tim – without another man in the house and, believe me, I know how bossy women can be.'

'I've got some good friends.'

'What about grandfathers?'

'One ... living in Norfolk.'

'That is a long way.' The pipe was carefully packed and relit. '"Tad- cu" means nothing to someone who does not speak Welsh,' the old man continued, 'so why not call me "Gramp". Then, you see, I could be your honorary grandfather while you are with us. That way you can bring any problems to me without worrying whether you should be bothering me or not. That way I will not be a stranger.'

Tim tossed his cigarette end into the fire and drank. There really was only one answer he could give and, at least, it settled the problem of names.

'Yes; I'd like to call you "Gramp".'

'Good; … now you and I are going to have another whisky, Tim. …You have shared your loss with me and I have a loss to share with you.'

Tim lay on his bed looking up at the ceiling which seemed to be moving. He raised himself up on his elbows and propped his head uncomfortably against the wall. His new-found grandfather's inquisition had been draining and he had not been able to escape the old man's dire news about his son. The problem had been to find appropriate words of sympathy and then to say them in a dignified manner. There he reckoned to have messed up. The old boy, hopefully as boozed as he was, hadn't seemed to be bothered by his slurred responses. … The bleak truth was that Mam was a widow; her husband killed by a rolling tractor on the high ground a number of years before. It seemed that the family's welfare depended almost entirely upon her son Geraint in the running of the farm and, to a small extent, himself and his weekly payments for bed and board. … He reached into his breast pocket for Rhyd's letter and opened it: …

*15 November 1958*                    *Wadham College*
                                            *Oxford*

*What Ho, Tim;*

*Everything's going mad up here. Parties every night and I've made lots of friends already. Cartloads of books have been chucked at me but there's damn all time to read them. Must get down to it sometime but a lot of distractions – one in particular – gorgeous girl from Somerville. She's also reading History. We got together on our first essays but it's not all work with us as I leave you to imagine. I can't quite believe my luck sometimes! It's beginning to look as though I may get picked for the college eight but I won't know for certain until next term. In the meantime I've been taking Lydia punting in all weathers to work off the booze and keep myself vaguely fit. I'm writing this in haste in my room; you know – the one with low rafters – and I still keep banging my head! I sent this to your home address hoping your mother would forward it. Write and let me know what the hell you're doing wherever you are. I hope you're having some fun. James wrote the other day. He's having a great time at Durham; a bit like here, only colder. ... Must dash – Lydia's waiting!*

*Yours Aye...Rhyd*

Tim put the letter down. It had left him feeling miserable and, worse still, jealous. Rhyd was having the time of his life; and he had found a girlfriend pretty damn quick; and he was rubbing it in. ... What chance was there of finding a girl here – in the back of beyond with people who, most of the time, spoke another language. ... It all came down to bloody money or the lack of it; and missing his last year in school. ... It had happened so quickly. He had been plucked out of the powerful stream which had carried his friends on to universities. Land agency had been an accident as far as he was concerned; urged upon him by his grandfather who, after a lifetime's work, had ended up in an Estate house he did not own.

His head was beginning to hurt. He sat up and fumbled in his pocket. There was only one cigarette left. He reached for the matches but they weren't there. He cursed, knowing he had left them downstairs. He crawled to the electric fire, turned it on and lay beside it, waiting to ignite the fag on its dimly glowing bar. He stood up unsteadily, supporting himself against the wall, turned off the light and went to the window. He dropped the sash and leaned out. A black November wind was raging against the big tree, making its branches creak. Tim felt that the weather was in sympathy with him; that jealousy was turning to anger. .... Rhyd's old man had received a flesh wound and picked up an MC. James's dad had spent the war in the navy, escorting convoys. They had survived. ... Tim rubbed his eyes and blinked against the wind. The whisky was bringing with it an uneasy truth – that, due to circumstances of wealth and geography, his path in life had irrevocably divided from those of his closest friends; the boys he had fought with, built dens with, fished with, boated with, shot with, chased girls with and built cars with. ... Nothing would be the same again. ... There had been an intimation of this at Wadham. Rhyd's parents had suggested he join them on their trip up to Oxford at the beginning of Rhyd's first term. There, the honeyed stone of the college quad, the stained glass windows of its darkened chapel and its lofty, antique dining hall had spoken to him not only of centuries of scholarship but also of the thousands of friendships made; connections which would linger for lifetimes; an unseen thread joining the alumni of that beautiful place; a brotherhood assisting its privileged companions to fame and fortune. ... The worst had been helping Rhyd to unpack in his room. Other recently arrived students, the sharers of his staircase, had kept noisily butting in and introducing themselves. With Rhyd it had ended with a casual wave as he disappeared through a stone archway in ardent conversation with new-found friends. Returning here had been hard. ...

Tim was annoyed to find himself crying, tears being blown across his face. He rubbed them away angrily, took a last draw on his cigarette and threw the stub out of the window. For a moment the wind trapped it and the dying glow of its ash against the wall of the house before releasing it to the darkness below. A gust crashed against the window, its cold, damp freshness invading his nostrils and smelling of earth. He decided to leave the window open. It was making him feel better but what he needed was a pee. He swayed to the bed, knelt down, groped for the chamber pot, removed its lid and relieved himself for what seemed an age. The problem now was to get rid of its contents undetected. He went to the window, cursing as he stumbled and banged the pot against the washstand. He leaned out, reached down and discharged the piss which promptly blew against the wall of the house. He cursed again, retrieved the pot, put it on the washstand, poured water into it and repeated the manoeuvre. He drank thirstily from the jug and looked around him. His eyes had got used to the dark. The bed and the rectangle of the sampler above it were visible in the gloom.

# CHAPTER 4

Tim's awakening had been a miserable affair. He had found himself sprawled on the bed, fully clothed, the fire still on and the window wide open to the remains of the gale. The linoleum below had been soaked by overnight rain. He had done his best to mop up with his flannel, wringing it out into the bowl. As he drove to work he hoped that Beth hadn't noticed. She'd slipped the jug of hot water round the door as usual but he hadn't heard her knock. Nothing had been said. In fact Mam had spent most of breakfast fussing over him. She had carved an extra slice of salt bacon off the flitch hanging from the ceiling and dropped it into the frying pan in spite of his protests. Beth had brought him a second mug of tea and patted him gently on the head. … As he turned right onto the main road his headache was beginning to ease but his encounter with Gramp had opened a wound. Self-pity was something he had always been taught to despise. He felt he was in danger of becoming a wet; an object of compassion. …

As he hurried into reception the girls peeped over their screens and grinned at him; he grinned back sheepishly and quickened his pace. This form of greeting had evolved into a habit over the weeks since his arrival.

Eleri called out. 'The Brig wants to see you.' Tim nervously consulted his watch. He was on time … just. The Brig seemed to be in a remarkably good mood though, in truth, the depth and number of his wrinkles made it hard to tell whether he was smiling or scowling; a fact which Tim had found disconcerting. The Brig stood up and handed him a plan. 'This one's six inches to the mile; ideal size. It's time you went somewhere without a nurse-maid.'

'What do you want me to do, sir?'

'Wait boy,' the Brig snapped; 'what you have there is a boundary plan of a farm belonging to the Twll Estate. The tenant is an odd fellow.'

'In what way odd, sir?'

'He's a machinery buff; loves old engines; he's got quite a collection. Don't get side-tracked or you'll be there all day.'

'Is there anything wrong with this plan, sir?' Tim ventured, trying to sound intelligent.

'No, there bloody well isn't; taken off the estate deeds. ... Now I want you to walk the boundaries with him and check that there are no invasions by neighbours. There have been rumours about one of em – a very unreliable fellow, by all accounts; and right on the edge of the estate.' The Brig pointed at the plan. 'You see that the boundaries are marked in blue. Any hanky- panky I want you to carefully mark in red and report back to me; not the tenant. My intelligence has been coming from locals who think he's being taken advantage of. Check the brook particularly. You'll note that our boundary is on the far side.'

'When do you want me to go, sir?'

'Today, of course; what do you think?'

'I have a bit of a problem, sir.'

'What problem?'

'My car is being serviced.'

'Damn and blast!' The Brig thought for a moment; then reached into his jacket pocket and produced a car key. 'Very well; you'll just have to take my car; and you'd better look after it.' ...

By half past ten Tim was on the road to Twll. The Brig's car, an ageing Ford Popular, had not taken to him or his way of driving. The gears were stubborn and the long lever seemed strangely detached from the workings of the box. Changes were frequently accompanied by a metallic cacophony. The engine, which whinnied like a sick horse at thirty miles an hour, howled in protest if he attempted to go over forty. ... Having lost his way on narrow lanes Tim arrived twenty-five minutes late. Farm buildings, in stone and tin were randomly grouped around a yard full of agricultural machinery. A stocky man in blue overalls with brown, curly hair – balding at the centre, came out of a large, corrugated iron shed with a half-round roof. The door clanged behind him in the breeze.

Apparently unaware of the time, the man extended his hand; then withdrew it, saying. 'It's covered in oil. I've been checking out "the big one." ...We'll pay her a visit after the other business, whatever it is.' He peered at the Ford Popular; then looked up at Tim. 'Is that your car?'

'Oh no,' said Tim, embarrassed at the very thought; 'It's the Brigadier's. Mine's being serviced.'

'I couldn't believe that someone like you would drive a car like that. You'd be better off with a horse and cart.' Tim was thinking of a suitable reply but the man got in first. 'You're not Welsh, are you?'

'I'm half Welsh actually,' replied Tim defensively.

The man laughed. 'Don't worry, lad. I'm English; a north-erner through and through; moved here after the war; cheaper land to rent, you see; and my good neighbours have taught me some Welsh so now I'm beginning to sound like them. … How about some Welsh cakes and a cup of tea?'

'I don't think I'll have time,' said Tim, mindful of the Brig's warning.

'Won't take long. My wife's just made some. Come up to the house.'

It had taken an hour to persuade the tenant to walk the boundaries with him. The interlude had not been dull. The tenant's wife was taller than her husband; and elegant in an un-showy way which spoke of a frail Anglo- Saxon gentility. She was someone Mother would have been happy to know but she was much younger than Mother. Over his mug of tea and the tales of farm machinery and its uses, with which the tenant was clearly obsessed, Tim had found himself glancing sideways at her, briefly taking in her pale complexion, her deep green eyes, her golden red pre-Raphaelite hair held in a silver clip and drifting down her back in a long pony tail. How had she ended up here – in the uplands above Twll with this jolly man who, on the face of things, was no match for her? Tim had looked about him for toys or sounds of children but there were none. She had said little; gently interrupting her talkative husband only to offer more tea or Welsh cakes – deliciously warm confections of floured sweetness and spice. Each time she had leaned towards him with the plate Tim had caught a whiff of her perfume - exotic and refined. …

The tenant had stopped walking and was pointing down at a section of fence which had strayed across a brook for a short distance of its running. 'That's probably what the Brigadier's worried about. It's not much and the poor fellow needs somewhere for his cattle to drink. See, the bank's scarred on his side. That's where they come down.' Tim nodded and marked the plan. They walked on. The tenant had, at last, stopped talking. Here, up in the hills at the beginning of winter, the countryside seemed busy. Brown water in the brook was crackling over boulders; the mournful call of a curlew was coming from the higher ground and, ahead of them, three snipe had broken from a patch of reeds at the centre of a wet field and were squawking into a wind blown sky. ...

Back on the farmyard Tim felt he had done well. He had identified two boundary incursions; both involving the brook. He was carefully marking the plan when the tenant interrupted ... 'I hope that the Brigadier won't be too hard on him. He's not a bad man though there are some round here that don't see eye to eye with him.' Tim, unwilling to commit the Brig to any kind of forbearance, nodded but remained silent.

'Now,' said the tenant, clapping his hands, 'you must come and see my oil engine. She's a beauty.' The engine was housed in the shed with the half-round roof. Set upon a concrete plinth its long, black cylinder, tapering to one end, gleamed in the half light. Attached to the nearside was a massive flywheel. The tenant was in full flow – describing its origins; how he had rescued it for next to nothing from a scrap yard; how a belt from a pulley on the far side would power heaven-knows-what machinery in the adjacent building by way of a drive shaft. He paused briefly; then looked up at Tim. 'Do you want to know how she works?' Tim nodded politely. 'Well she runs on oil because she's an oil engine; tremendous compression to ignite the stuff. She only fires when she feels the need. The rest is up to the flywheel. When that gets going there's no stopping her … very economical.' The tenant reached under the machine and brought out a large crank handle. 'Would you like to have a go?' he asked, his dark eyes bright with enthusiasm.

Tim, frantically searching for a suitable reply, decided upon flattery. 'You're obviously the expert.'

'Very well,' said the tenant. He engaged the crank handle and started to turn the flywheel; slowly at first; then quickening the pace. The engine snorted and spat. A puff of black smoke came out of a small aperture at the narrow end and then a loud bang. Tim could see the tenant shooting upwards; a blur propelled by an unseen force. As the man's head hit the curved roof a sheet of tin opened to receive him to the sky; then closed again. … Tim was still looking up in amazement when there was a mighty crash above him. A slithering sound and a dull thud indicated that the man was back on his yard – but in what condition? Tim turned and made for the door. It opened before he could get to it – framing the figure of the tenant, patting himself down.

'Are you alright?' asked Tim, anxiously; reaching out to him.

'Fine,' said the tenant, limping into the building; 'a bruise or two may-be. … It's not the first time.'

'You mean it's happened before?'

'Oh yes', said the man, nonchalantly, 'in September –

shortly after I'd installed her.' Rubbing his head and looking upwards, he continued; 'it's a blessing I didn't fix that piece of roof cladding. It's in just the right place. ... Look – after all that she's running.' In the hubbub Tim had failed to notice the slow thud of the engine and the rotation of its flywheel. The man went over to the machine, made a few adjustments to screws at the tapered end and stood back to admire his handywork. 'There,' he exclaimed, 'she's running like a watch now.' He patted the cylinder, beamed at Tim and shouted above the noise. 'She can be a bitch at times but she's a good girl really.'

On the way back to the office Tim had arrived at an uneasy truce with the Ford Popular upon the strict condition that he did not exceed thirty-five miles per hour. He was reflecting upon the day's events. Things hadn't gone badly – apart from the bloody near shave he'd had with the engine. Only now was it dawning upon him that he could have said yes to cranking it and ended up in hospital or on a slab. The man must have been made of rubber! ... And his wife was a mystery; a lily-flower in a muddy pond but she seemed content. It was none of his business but he knew that the subtle memory of her would remain with him. He had felt immediately attracted to her and the poignancy of her situation. A few unspoken signs of affection; a smile, a sideways glance, a gentle touch on his sleeve were hardly enough to suggest that his feelings had been shared. He was beginning to feel ashamed of his thoughts. After all her husband seemed a good man; permanently optimistic and without guile; a fellow who could maintain and cherish an evil-tempered, antique cow of an engine which would regularly blow him out of the building in which it was housed. ... May'be that was it – the caring; the patience. ... He wondered whether there would be an opportunity to revisit the farm; to see her again; to satisfy his curiosity; but her strange juxtaposition would probably remain a puzzle ...

His daydreaming was brought to a halt by a tractor coming towards him, filling the lane. He fought with the gear lever, trying to obey the diagram on its knob until the cogs engaged with a clunk which sent the car backwards in kangaroo leaps to the nearest gateway. The tractor driver grinned and waved as he passed. Tim depressed the clutch pedal and attempted to change into first; then second; but the gear lever was stuck.

Two hours later Tim entered reception, coming face to face with the Brig, puce with rage.'Where the hell have you been?' he shouted; 'any longer and I'd have sent a search and rescue party. I need my car!'

'There's been a problem, sir.'

'What damned problem?'

'Your car, sir. ... It's jammed in gear sir.'

'What!' The Brig paused for a moment, his eyes narrowing in undisguised hostility. 'You bloody boy. You've mangled my gearbox! ... Which gear are you stuck in?'

'Reverse, sir.'

'You mean I'll have to spend the rest of my time going around the county in a permanent state of retreat!' There was stifled laughter from behind the screens. The Brig swung round. 'Silence,' he bellowed to the unseen faces; 'this is no laughing matter. Get on with your work!'

'I'm really sorry about it, sir,' said Tim, not wanting to be blamed for the deficiencies of the Brig's motor; 'but I don't think it's my fault.'

'Of course it is, boy,' snarled the Brig, rounding on him; 'The problem with all you young whipper-snappers is an absence of double-declutching.'

Tim, feeling that a helpless descent into laughter was imminent, fought to compose himself. 'It's in a garage, sir. ... I wasn't far from a house. I phoned and got towed in.'

'Which garage?'

'The one that I took my car to this morning. ... "James and somebody ….. ;" I forget the other name, sir.'

'That's one good thing. James knows the car at least.'

'Yes sir. He said he could fix it. ... He did mention that it's had this problem before, sir.'

'Yes', the Brig retorted, 'in the hands of those lacking the patience to treat her with proper respect. ... If they can't get my car back on the road by tomorrow then I'll simply have to borrow yours; and I want your report on what you've been up to by nine hundred hours tomorrow.'

Tim left the office, appalled at the idea of the Brig being allowed to abuse his precious Minor. He apprehensively walked down to the garage at the bottom of the hill, a ramshackle collection of tin and concrete buildings. The cracked glass domes over the three petrol pumps flickered dimly in the light of a winter afternoon. The real business of repair went on in a dark, soot-stained and hellish-looking interior. Tim was greeted by the proprietor, a large, genial man in filthy, oil-stained overalls and who, by common consent, could work mechanical miracles.

'She's ready to take away,' he said, pointing to the Minor parked beside one of the sheds.

'What about the Ford?'

'Don't worry; I've bounced her out. I'll drive her up to the Brigadier tomorrow. ... To tell the truth I cannot think why he holds onto her. She should be on a dump, Mr Tim.'

'"Mr" makes me sound a bit old,' said Tim, warming to the man.

'Too late; everybody knows you as "Mr Tim,"' said the big man. 'Rhywle is a place where you can keep a secret for all of ten minutes. ... I hope you think I am respectful enough.'

'You think I'm respectable then?'

'I hope so,' exclaimed the man, doubling up in mirth; laughing with the voice of a high tenor; 'but, if not, we'll soon find out!'

As Tim drove up the hill he was still smiling. There were things to be happy about. His day had been anything but boring and he would be able to give a full report to the Brig in the morning.

# CHAPTER 5

Mother stood in the hall admiring herself in the large oval mirror. She adjusted her hat and secured it with a pin. 'There, I think the ribbon sets it off very nicely.' She turned to Sophie. 'What do you think, darling?'

'Mother, we're going to a farmyard.'

'I know dear; but we mustn't let Tim down.'

'We'll embarrass him. ... Must I wear this ridiculous hat?'

'I would be very disappointed if you didn't. It goes so well with that skirt and top.'

'I think the whole thing makes me look middle-aged.'

'On the contrary, I think you look very charming. Tim will be proud of you.'

'What will his landlady think?'

'Believe me, darling, she'll be dressing up for us.'

In this Sophie could perceive a truth; that hospitality in these rural backwaters, although lacking in sophistication, was akin to a religion and that no effort would be spared to honour the visitor. The gallons of tea taken from broad-brimmed cups and the many cakes consumed in damp parlours during her childhood visits with mother to local farms and homesteads on behalf of The British Legion and the Sunday-School had taught her that. ... 'Shall I tell him?'

'Tell him what?'

'My news.'

'Of course; why not?'

'It might upset him.'

'Nonsense; ... he'll be proud of you.'

Sophie thought for a moment. 'Is he really happy – with Rhydian and James away?'

'He hasn't told me otherwise.'

'Well he wouldn't, would he. He must be lonely living and working in that place. ... He can't speak Welsh either.'

'He's learning, which I think is very courageous of him.'

'I got a letter from him at school but it didn't tell me much; no mention of any friends.'

'That's why we're going to visit; to see what sort of people he's with.' Mother hesitated. 'Has he told you he's unhappy?'

'No; but you know him; he wouldn't want to bother me.'

'He's here most weekends and he hasn't said anything.' Mother paused. 'You have got the letter?'

'Yes - in my handbag.' ...

Tim was sitting at his table finishing his essay on farm building maintenance. He reckoned he'd made a good job of it. What he had picked up from the study notes had been amplified by practical advice from Geraint and Gramp who, it seemed, were taking a lively interest in the agricultural side of his tutoring. He pinned the papers together and placed them into the brown, foolscap envelope provided. Mother and Sophie could post it on their way home. ... Their proposal to call at short notice had created pandemonium. Mam had been baking cakes all morning. Beth had spent most of the day cleaning and besoming everything in sight in spite of the fact that the house was already a stranger to dust.

Gramp, who had been grumbling extensively about the fuss, had been shoo'd away to the farmyard. Now he was back and raising his voice in complaint. Tim went downstairs to investigate. The corridor leading to the parlours was filling up with large, high-backed chairs of different designs and complexity. Gramp, standing near the front door, was pointing. 'Look at all these, Tim. What are they doing – buggering about like this?' Mam emerged backwards from the parlwr mawr, carrying what looked like an oaken throne, supported at the other end by Beth. They placed it alongside the others. Mam straightened up and glared at Gramp. 'That's the last of them … and I am out of breath; much help you are!'

'Tim's mother and sister would fit very well into the parlwr bach to be sure,' Gramp retorted.

'No they would not; it is too small. We'd be like kippers in a box.'

'What about the kitchen then? It is the most comfortable place in the house.'

'Mam,' Tim interrupted, 'the kitchen will be fine.'

'No it won't. It would not be fitting.'

The expression on Mam's face told Tim that further argument was out of the question. He decided to change the subject. 'These chairs; they're very grand. Where did they come from?'

Mam sat down on one of them, breathing heavily. 'Hasn't he told you already?'

'Who?'

'Tac; … he won them all at Eisteddfodau. They are bardic chairs.'

'You mean – for poetry.'

'Yes; the best part of him if you should ask me. If he wins any more we'll have to live on the yard.'

Tim looked at Gramp. … 'Why didn't you tell me?'

'I didn't think you would be interested; a young lad like you. …. All my poems are in Welsh, you see, and…'

'Tac, you can tell Tim about it later,' Mam interrupted. 'Now you go and get into your best. You know how long you take.'

'Do I have to? It's bad enough on Sundays; a real bugger.'

'You mind your language. I want none of that in front of the ladies.'

'Does your sister look like you?' asked Beth, her dark, passive eyes suddenly inquisitive.

Tim began to wonder whether, to Beth, he appeared effeminate. Certainly Geraint and Gramp were hardy, rural types; so was a swarthy, taciturn man who would occasionally call upon her. He considered his reply carefully. 'Not really.'

'Come on Beth,' said Mam. 'We have got to clean up in there and light a fire. Then we must get ourselves ready.'

'What shall I wear?' asked Beth, vacantly.

'I'm sure my mother isn't expecting all this,' said Tim.

'I think you will find that she is', replied Mam firmly.

An hour later Tim was up in his room. As the whole household, including Gramp, were being required to dress up for his mother and sister he had decided to join them. He was standing at the mirror, in his cavalry- twill trousers and tweed jacket, brushing his hair when he heard Mother's clarion voice on the yard. He peered through the window. In the twilight Sophie looked like a traffic light in cherry red. Mother was in a white coat and a broad hat and looked like a film star. Tim groaned. He saw Mam come out to meet them – her dark, silvering hair done up in its usual bun. Her long winter skirt and plain top, the kit she wore to Chapel, seemed more suited to the occasion but Tim noticed that she was wearing a white apron. Was this a sign of servitude; that her only function was to wait upon them? Gramp had told him, during one of several conversations by the fire, of the ways of Welsh matrons – serving the needs of others with little thought for themselves. Tim took a deep breath and went downstairs to join them.

Two hours later Mother and Sophie were sitting on the bed. Tim sat in the low armchair.

'This bed is very hard,' said Mother. 'How on earth do you sleep on it?'

'I've got used to it.'

'Amazing,' cried Sophie, bouncing up and down; 'I could never, ever sleep on this; the mattress is full of lumps; poor you!'

Tim looked up. Sophie's cornflower blue eyes were studying him through the net of a red velvet toque. It seemed that, within the course of a school term, his sister had slipped unnoticed into womanhood; her light auburn hair up in combs, her slender neck, her skin unblemished, her features delicate and refined. Gone was the girl he had tormented and who had tormented him; whose pigtails he had pulled, whom he had run through the woods with, whom he had chased around the garden and built dens with, who had shrieked all the way to the dentist, whose spots he had mocked; who, on mother's instructions, he had had to dance with when she was a "wallflower." ... There would be no shortage of partners now. Tim sensed a boundary, unseen and unintended; never to be crossed again. 'You're wearing a hat,' he said.

'It was Mother's idea. I look daft.' With a swift movement of her small hands she removed the hat and plonked it on the bed. 'I felt like a caged bird in there!'

Mother patted her knee. 'Thank you, darling, for wearing it until now. You looked a real picture in it.'

'God knows what they thought downstairs. I felt like the Queen Mother!'

'You made a very good impression, I'm sure.' Mother paused and looked at Tim. 'Mrs Davies; ... why do you call her Mam? I thought that was reserved for Royalty.'

'It's like "Mum" in Welsh. May'be it's the way I say it.'

'She's very sweet and hospitable,' Mother continued, 'but the daughter does seem a bit vacant. As for the old man I think he's rather disreputable.'

'That's what it may look like,' said Tim, leaping to Gramp's defence; 'but there's more to him than meets the eye. He's a Bard; a poet!'

'Is he published?' asked Mother, brightening.

'I guess so. He's won a lot of Eisteddfod prizes. All those chairs down there are his and ...'

'What! In the corridor?' Sophie interrupted.

'Yes.'

'Odd place to keep them.'

'They were taken out of the room we had tea in.'

'My God!' Sophie cried. 'They shouldn't have bothered. It

67

was so musty in there. ...That sofa's left me with a damp bottom.'

'Don't be common,' snapped Mother. ... 'Tim, is there anywhere I can buy his books?'

'You wouldn't be able to read them, Mother. They're in Welsh.'

Mother, feeling disappointed that Gramp's behaviour was not a cloak for a literary genius to whom she had access and about whom she might talk with her friends, continued; 'Mrs Davies, your "Mam" had to apologise for him on a number of occasions for saying ... well I can't say...'

'He said "bugger" a lot, Mother.'

'Sophie, I never want to hear that word on your lips.'

Tim intervened. 'It doesn't mean what you think it means, Mother.'

'What?'

'"Bugger" around here seems to refer to some general annoyance or even a term of endearment. People say it to each other all the time.'

Sophie had begun to snigger. Mother was looking thoughtful. 'Tim dear, I do hope that you won't be ... corrupted by him.'

'Don't be silly, Mother. He's been really kind to me. He told you, didn't he, that he's become my honorary Grandfather.'

'That is what is worrying me, dear.'

'Well don't. I think he deliberately puts up a bit of a front for strangers; teases them a little. It was the same for me until we got talking. Now he's helping with my agricultural papers and my Welsh. He's cleverer than you think and he knows just about everybody.'

'He offered to put whisky in my tea, of all things,' said Mother, looking uneasy; 'and he put some in yours and you drank it!'

'It's really very good in cold weather; warms you up.'

Mother paused and glanced at Sophie. 'Sophie's got some news, Tim. Show him the letter, darling.'

'I can tell him, Mother. ... I've been awarded an open exhibition to St Hilda's; reading English!'

Tim jumped up and hugged his sister; he was breathing a perfume he had not encountered before. 'That's wonderful, Soph; really wonderful!'

'Such good news', said Mother, 'but there should be no slacking, Sophie darling; there's many a slip.'

'But I still have to endure practically a whole year, Mother.'

'You're deputy head girl. That can't be bad.'

'It doesn't help with the head girl being such a drip.' ...

'You'll have to be patient.'

'I just know it's going to be a real bore.'

Tim was beginning to feel detached – his eyes closing. Mother patted his leg. 'You're dropping off on us! ... We must be going anyway. The Vicar's calling at eight o'clock.' Mother hesitated; 'Tim dear, I hate to ask you this but you didn't put anything in our "Bring and Buy" box the weekend before last, did you?' Mother's grey-green eyes, shielded by the brim of her hat, were fixing him. He decided to avoid the question

'What thing?'

Mother's reply was stumbling. 'Rather unpleasant, embarrassing things. ... I don't really want to say ....'

'"French letters", Sophie cut in; 'lots of them!'

'Sophie!' Mother exclaimed; 'you really shouldn't know about such things and you certainly shouldn't talk about them!'

'Mother; next year I'll be in Oxford.'

'That does not give you licence to be lewd. ... Tim, you do know what I'm talking about, don't you?'

Tim blushed and, feeling himself to be at a junction of shame, guilt and mirth, sought to change the direction of Mother's inquisition. 'Where were they found?'

'In the box of things I took from the house. Heaven knows how they got there! Perhaps someone casually dropped them in at the hall. The box was unpacked by Sandra; you know – the church cleaner's daughter and she's old enough to know better. She put them on the stall she was running without any consultation whatsoever.'

'It gets worse, Tim,' said Sophie, stifling laughter; peering at him through damp fingers.

'It's no laughing matter,' Mother continued; 'the whole thing was deeply unfortunate. You know old Miss Jenkins of Church Cottage; takes the collection every Sunday. Well she's practically blind with those pebble glasses of hers and she bought several of the "boxes." Apparently she thought that they were some special kind of tea and ....'

'And you know what happened then,' cried Sophie, falling back on the bed, abandoned to hysterics; 'she took them home, unpacked one of them and dropped it into her teapot!' Tim could hold back no longer and, when the laughter came, it wouldn't stop, doubling him up.

'You two are finding this all very amusing,' continued

Mother unabated; 'but what about poor Miss Jenkins?'

Tim couldn't resist the question. 'Did she drink any of the "tea"?'

'If you should ask me Sophie's been listening to some very unkind exaggerations. ... Obviously she knew something was wrong. She took them all to the Vicar.'

'What did he do with them,' asked Tim, wanting to continue with the diversion.

'God knows. He told me he'd refunded her what she had paid and left it at that. Any explanation would have been deeply distressing for the poor old thing.'

Sophie sat up, rubbing her eyes. 'Do you think he's kept them?'

'Who?'

'The Vicar.'

'That's an impertinent question, Sophie,' Mother retorted; 'you know very well that he's unmarried. I would imagine he's thrown the things away already.'

'Perhaps he's put them on his bonfire.'

Tim glanced up at his sister – wanting to join in the fun. 'But Soph, the smell of burning rubber would be all over the Parish.'

'Then perhaps he's put them in the bin.'

'What if the bin men found them?'

'They'd think he was some kind of maniac,' Sophie blurted; 'I bet he's kept them for ...'

'Now that's enough of that, you two,' Mother snapped; 'you aren't taking the situation at all seriously.'

Tim looked up at his mother, whose face had creased into a reluctant smile. 'But it's an amusing situation, Mother. You must admit.'

'May'be for you; but not for Miss Jenkins. She must be totally bewildered.'

'It seems she's none the wiser.'

'Thank God for that. ... You look tired, Tim. Is it the work?'

'It's alright,' Tim replied, happy that Mother had changed the subject. He pointed at the table, loaded with papers; 'but I've got those to get through tonight.'

'Well I think you're very brave, Tim dear – tackling all this together. I've never heard you complain.'

'There's nothing to complain about. You really mustn't worry about me. ... I'll get through it; you'll see.'

Mother stood up, her expression suddenly changed. 'Oh Tim,' she whispered, 'you looked and sounded so like your father just then; almost the very words he said to me when we parted for the last time.' ... Tim stood for her embrace. Sophie was wiping away tears which were no longer those of laughter.

Later that evening Tim was lying on his bed. He had spent upwards of three hours reading the study notes and he had had enough. The visit had, at least, gone off without major embarrassments. Mam's tea had been too generous with ham and jam sandwiches, fruit cakes, sponge cakes – even raspberry jelly on offer. Mother and Sophie had made little impression upon this cornucopia and he had felt duty bound to make up for it. Having declined supper in favour of work, he still felt bloated. ... Mam and Beth had spent all of the time on their feet, unwilling to sit down; constantly offering the many plates around and scuttling to and from the kitchen. This had left Gramp as the only member of the household with whom a coherent conversation could be carried on. He had, in the event, been just himself, telling stories of local characters and their proclivities; staying just the right side of what Mother would have deemed proper. In the process he had won Sophie over – making her laugh out loud, much to Mother's discomfiture, on a number of occasions. The smoking fire had annoyed him – a damp glow surrounded by a hideous tiled surround and mantel. Several times he had cursed it in English and in Welsh, jabbing at the smouldering ruin with a long brass poker. He was right, of course. They would have been far better off around the big log fire under the open chimney. At one point he had suggested that the whole party decamp to the kitchen but Mam was having none of it.

Tim reached for the packet of ten and the box of matches. He lit a cigarette, went to the window and dropped the sash. The night was cold. In the light of a full moon, which had cleared the summit of Twll Hill, the tree was casting its shadow over the yard, the pattern of its branches clearly defined. The fields beyond shone silver. There was no sound except an occasional stirring of cattle in the sheds at the bottom of the yard. … The matter of the French letters had been a near shave but, in the event, he could not have done better. The shame of his deception had been expunged by laughter. Tim drew on his cigarette. If he had told Mother the whole story of how he had rescued Teg as an act of Christian charity she would never have believed him. She would have thought that he was covering up some unmentionable vice. He chuckled, stubbed out the cigarette against the window sill and watched its dying glow drift down to the yard. He reached for the packet and lit another. ... Soph's news had not been a total surprise. She had always been brighter than him – producing spectacular exam results with apparently minimum effort compared to his plodding. Mother would not have to bury her pride and apply for a grant. Soph would walk into Oxford with all guns blazing and open doors to a future full of attractive options and opportunities. ... Tim drew heavily on his cigarette. ... Perhaps Soph and Rhyd would meet up. She had never really liked him thinking him too cocky; but, in those romantic surroundings, they might even fall for each other. Tim laughed out loud at the thought. He turned away, went to the bedside cabinet, groped inside and found the half bottle of whisky. He poured himself a good measure and topped it up with water from the jug. He switched off the light, returned to the window and sipped at the warming spirit. ... Mother's emotional parting embrace had taken him by surprise; had left him feeling inadequate; dry-eyed. On her bedroom wall hung a photograph taken before she and father had married. They had looked so happy; he, in a blazer and boater, at the wheel of an open lagonda and she, in a white, flowing blouse and scarf; head thrown back in abandon; her blonde hair flowing; her sleeve draped carelessly down to the running board.

# CHAPTER 6

The Reverend Ebenezer Jones woke to a blur, groped for his spectacles and silenced his alarm clock. He sank back onto the pillows and groaned, focussing upon the window in front of him. A pale dawn was lighting up the heights of Twll Hill and the sun would soon break free of its horizon. In winter, on a clear day, when the sun was low, he reckoned to be able, almost, to tell the day of the year from the vantage point of his bed. The trick was to relate the first shaft of warm light to certain rocks upon the skyline. ... Today was a Sunday, the third before Christmas. He sighed, reached out and stroked a large, brindled cat which lay curled up beside him. The animal stretched and purred. Samuel was a good cat and he had loved Elinor as well as any creature could. Ebenezer closed his eyes. Christmas was a time for counting your blessings not licking your wounds; and there had been many blessings. Forty years she had put up with him through thick and thin and that was a job in itself. Together they had built up a tidy congregation. Upon his retirement the Elders had organised a testimonial of such generous proportions that, with the money scraped and saved over the years, they had been able to buy this modest, grey stone house. Even in her short retirement her hands had always been busy. Ebenezer looked to the right of the window. Her last sampler had been her best; a labour of love and faith accomplished in declining health. With all manner of stitching, patterns and colours she had mimicked the little house and its fruitful garden under the words "Jesus Saves." … Very appropriate, for he himself had been rescued from self-pity and despair by frequent consultation of the scriptures. … For sure she was now with the elect.

Ebenezer sat up and scratched his head. Today there was much to do; tea to make, breakfast to eat, Chapel to go to; a reading from the Old Testament and, afterwards, meeting the young Englishman Tac Morgan had told him about and who wanted to learn Welsh. That, in itself, was a cause for rejoicing. … Then it would be back home to clear the greenhouse of its old pots and rubbish before the light failed.

Gramp, in a tight-fitting black suit, white shirt and wing collar chafing at the wrinkles of his neck, stood with Tim in front of the uncompromising rectangle of stone, brick and stucco that was Jabez Chapel. They had walked there – persuaded by the rare stillness and clarity of a winter morning. Gramp had already been drawn into close conversation with early arrivals, speaking in Welsh. Tim moved away. He began to examine the facade in the detailed manner prescribed by his study papers. Near the apex he spotted a date stone reading "1837". Tall windows were set above a wide central doorway with smaller doorways to left and right. Above each of these a word in Welsh had been incised into the fabric. The arches over door and window openings suggested a primitive elegance. … He felt a tap on his shoulder.

'Does this dull old place interest you, Tim?' There was a suggestion of surprise in Gramp's voice.

'I … I was wondering what the words meant.'

'Which words?'

'Over the doorways.'

Gramp grinned wickedly at him and pointed. 'Ahh; now that one reads "Men" and the other one reads "Women." In the old days they were supposed to keep themselves apart during the services; to concentrate upon the scriptures and not the lusts of the flesh. Very few bother these days; only some of the old fashioned buggers who are past it anyway and are just doing it for show.' Gramp was heading for the main door. 'We had better get to my pew before any other bugger takes it.' Tim was led to a vacant pew in the front row. A wooden pulpit reared above them. Gramp sat down with a groan and parked his stick.

'Do we need to be this close?' Tim whispered.

'If we are not up the front I can hear bugger all. The place echoes like hell,' muttered Gramp, whose attention seemed to be elsewhere. 'She does not look very happy.'

'Who?'

'Megan; the organist. She usually plays them in; likes to show off.'

A small pipe organ was installed beneath the balcony forward and to the right of them. A frail, bird-like woman, wrapped in a heavy, woollen coat and wearing a hat which reminded Tim of one of Mother's sponge cakes, sat hunched over the keys, her hands buried in a muff. Beyond her a door opened and she was joined by a plump, well groomed man in a black suit. …

'The Minister,' said Gramp; 'something is up for sure.'

'Perhaps the organ's broken down.'

'Possibly; … she is an awkward old cow; but I cannot see Twm the pump.'

Tim had become aware that the Minister was observing him and looked away.

'Damn it to hell! Tim can you find the bloody thing?'

'What?'

'The bloody ear-piece; it never fitted properly. Those deaf doctors in the hospital probably mixed me up with someone else, the silly buggers. …'

Tim, anxious to avoid the stares of those sitting close in the aftermath of Gramp's explosion, was groping under the pew when the litany of abuse stopped abruptly – replaced by an apparently polite conversation in Welsh. He found the ear-piece between Gramp's brightly polished, black shoes and sat up. The Minister had joined them. Gramp gripped Tim by the arm. 'You will do it Tim, won't you?'

'Do what, Gramp?'

'Help out with the organ.'

Tim stood up in panic, desperately thinking of an excuse to leave. 'I …I really can't read music or play anything. I only got to grade two on the piano. Then I gave it up because I was no good. … '

'Don't worry,' said the Minister soothingly, putting his hand on Tim's shoulder; 'it's nothing like that. Come with me.' Tim was taken to the far side of the organ, out of sight of the congregation. The Minister was pointing at a lever projecting from a vertical slot in the wooden casing. 'It's simple really; you just have to keep Miss Jenkins supplied with wind.'

'Miss Jenkins?'

'The organist,' whispered the Minister, pumping the lever

up and down.'Slow and steady, you see; up and down, up and down when she's playing; and see this.' The Minister was pointing at a small lead weight suspended on a cord running over a pulley. A line had been scratched into the panelling below. 'The bellows have a leak somewhere we can't find,' the Minister continued, 'so rule one is always keep the lead below the line when you are pumping.'

'What happens if I don't?'

'The organ dies and Miss Jenkins gets very upset.'

'Has it happened before?'

'Occasionally, when Twm has lost his concentration. ... He's not the brightest of lads but, usually, very punctual.' The Minister looked at his watch. 'I can't imagine what's kept him today. ... It's good of you to help us out. An intelligent young man like you should have no trouble at all.'

'But I don't speak Welsh, Sir,' Tim protested; 'I won't know when to pump!'

'You can sit with Tac. He'll tell you when to come here – for the hymns and the psalm. He'll send you early each time to get the pressure up before Miss Jenkins starts playing; otherwise she goes out of tune or worse; and she's a perfectionist. If in doubt keep an eye on her. She'll keep you on the straight and narrow. ... Come on; I'll introduce you.'

Miss Jenkins had dark, suspicious eyes, enlarged by the powerful lenses of the tortoiseshell spectacles which clung to the end of her angular nose. Her hand felt frail in his and bony; her greeting seemed reluctant.


By the time they had got to the sermon Tim was feeling pleased with himself. He had mastered the pumping routine through three hymns and a psalm in spite of the fact that the bellows had hissed at him like an angry tom-cat seemingly intent upon deflation. Deep strokes of the handle were doing the trick and he had even extracted a weak smile from Miss Jenkins. Her hoarsely whispered advice had been to count the verses and wait for the "amen"; then let go. With apparently no direction the congregation had gone their own way in untutored harmony – filling the place with a solid sound, the volume of which had, at times, made the organ seem irrelevant. ... The singing in school chapel had never been as good as this; and Mother's church made a pitiful comparison – an uncertain congregation led by a whinnying choir of the elderly. Tim imagined that many came here for the singing and not the sermon which was being declaimed above him, which he could not understand and which seemed to be going on too long. He looked up. The Minister was in full flow, his voice pitched high, his face flushed, boyish and unlined save the crows feet around sharp eyes which fixed different parts of his congregation in turn. Tim reckoned that this was a good strategy to prevent anyone from dozing off. ... Sermons had always seemed too long at home, dragging him inevitably towards slumber and Mother's nudge. A prelude to sleep had, more often than not, been a perusal of the large plaque on the wall in front of their pew recording, in greatest detail, the exploits of Sir Anthony Carruthers-Lloyd in biffing the natives of far-off places in the name of God and Queen Victoria. Ironically, the loss of the one male heir in the war and swingeing taxes thereafter had dissolved the estate; most of its lands, houses and contents now gone. Mother was on social terms with the two surviving sisters who had retreated to the dower house. She had taken Tim to the big house auction of contents. There she had bought a few things in a gesture of support but which she had secretly suggested were bargains. ...

Tim felt Gramp's nudge and leapt to his feet; but the sermon hadn't ended; the Minister was speaking in English. Tim sat down again, his cheeks burning with embarrassment, as the Minister continued. 'I cannot finish without thanking the young gentleman for his valiant efforts in providing a bountiful supply of air to Miss Jenkins. We sincerely hope to see him again and I understand that he is to start Welsh lessons with my worthy predecessor. ... He could not be in better hands.' There was a murmur of approval from the rear and the gallery followed by a short round of applause. Tim was looking down at the floor, hoping to be swallowed up, feeling that he had made an exhibition of himself and wanting to be anything other than the centre of attention. ... Another nudge from Gramp and this time it was for hymn number four. ...

Tim had confidently pumped his way through the five verses down to what sounded like the "amen" and released the lever; but the congregation, for reasons known only to itself, continued to sing. He peeped around the corner at Miss Jenkins who was glaring at him, her clenched fist urging him on; but it was too late. The lead was above the line and the bright sound of the pipes had become the wheezing lamentation of a cow in search of a calf. Tim's face was on fire; but with anger, not shame. How the hell was he supposed to know that there was a sixth bloody verse? He jerked the lever savagely up and down, his tempo reflecting his mood. The organ began to throb erotically in time with his pumping. He checked with Miss Jenkins again. This time her left hand was extended – frantically waving him down. When the singing had ceased he carried on for fear that the congregation would pull a fast one again. By the time Miss Jenkins had left her seat and come round the corner to stop him, the prayers had begun. ...

He rejoined Gramp who was muttering angrily and adjusting the volume control on the box which was clipped into the top pocket of his jacket. The shrill, oscillating squawk from the ear-piece was drowning the Minister's devotions. Gramp thumped the box with his fist. Tim reached across and turned the volume down. The din ceased. Gramp leaned close. 'Tim, the bloody machine is wrong and I can't hear the bugger praying!' Gramp's remarkably loud observation had, unfortunately, occupied a brief pause in the proceedings. There was tittering from the balcony. Tim buried his head in his hands and peered upwards through the web of his fingers. The Minister was looking down at them, his rounded face in a half smile. The prayers continued. ...

The walk home was taking its time. The gradient and the need to catch his breath had imposed an untypical silence upon Gramp. When the service was over Tim had attempted to escape from the chapel unnoticed – leaving Gramp in conversation with the occupants of the neighbouring pew. He had been caught at the door by the Minister who had grabbed his hand and, before letting go, had apologised for not warning him that the congregation were frequently in the habit of singing the last verse more than once and that the hymn in question was one of their favourites. They had arrived at a turn in the lane where the hedge dipped to reveal the valley below. Gramp stopped, breathing heavily and leant on his stick. 'You did well there, Tim; with the organ; but they caught you out in the end.'

'Did they mean to?'

'No, of course not. … To tell the truth I have been to many funerals where last verses were sung three or even four times. Took ages to get the poor buggers into the ground.'

'Perhaps', said Tim thoughtfully, 'it's about not letting go.'

'Or people just love the sound of their own voices,' said Gramp, lashing at a bramble with his stick. … 'I may make a bard out of you yet.' … Gramp leaned forward and spat into the shallow ditch which lay between them and the hedge. Then he turned, a twinkle in his eye. 'Did the Minister say anything about me?'

'Do you really want to know?'

'Of course.'

'He said that I mustn't learn any bad habits from you.'

Gramp convulsed into coarse laughter, rocking to and fro over his stick. 'He is not a bad man. You know where you are with him.' The old man paused to draw breath. 'There was trouble with some of the old-fashioned buggers who were against me being an Elder but he supported me. He likes my poems, you see; so, fair play, I am happy to listen to him preaching.'

'What was he preaching about?'

'Salvation; … eternal life; and I thought it would never

end,' said Gramp, looking mischievous, the gap in his yellowing front teeth more obvious than usual. 'Do you think you are saved?'

'I don't know,' said Tim, not liking the turn of the conversation.

'You ought to be. You are a good enough lad.'

'What's it supposed to feel like?'

'Well, they keep telling us that a hell of some kind is just round the corner but what do you make of heaven?'

'I wouldn't know,' said Tim, embarrassed by his lack of opinion.

Gramp, undeterred by Tim's negativity, looked upwards at the pallid blue and white of a December sky and sighed. 'All this talk of harps and choirs of angels and being friendly with every bugger for ever and ever; ... it would drive me mad! If you should ask me there is the answer,' said Gramp, pointing over the hedge with his stick. ...

Tim looked down into the narrow valley. Its steep, wooded sides were linked by a level carpet of mist; an insubstantial field of light he felt he could walk upon; its tendrils working among the branches and, beyond, the high ground of central Wales crouched in a distant opacity. ... A feeling utterly incapable of description, luminous and uplifting, was stirring within him. ...

'Now there is a vision for you but it will be gone in minutes,' said Gramp, breaking the spell. 'I can feel a poem coming.'

'I've written a few of my own,' said Tim. His admission had been furtive. He was already hoping that Gramp hadn't heard him.

'Poems, Tim,' said Gramp, brightening. 'You must let me read them.'

'You wouldn't like them.'

'How do you know? Have you read them to anyone else?'

'No; ... not really.' ...

Tim was not going to admit to the one occasion when he had tried them out in a pub. Fired up by too much beer he had declaimed two, one after the other. Initially puzzled, Rhyd and James had been rendered prostrate by drunken laughter. The two girls they were with had been more restrained and had shown some interest but not the kind of interest he was looking for at the time. ...

'I can help you if you like, Tim.'

'But you're writing in Welsh.'

'Poetry is just another way of thinking – in any language'

'But I couldn't read yours.'

'Remember, you will be learning Welsh before long, you poor bugger.'

'Is he a good teacher?' asked Tim, spotting an opportunity to head off Gramp's growing interest in his pitiful output.

'Who?'

'The Reverend Jones.' Tim had detected an unspoken zeal in the intensely blue eyes of the tall and stooping man they had met up with after the service in the chapel yard. The conversation, in deference to himself, had been in English and Gramp had been untypically reticent; respectful even.

'Ebenezer is a good man,' replied Gramp thoughtfully; 'lives by the Bible and fixed in his ways; a very spiritual individual if you should ask me. ... Be warned though; he may ask you if you are a Christian.' Gramp hesitated; 'You are, aren't you?'

'I suppose so.'

'Just as well. He may try to save you anyway; so look out –
fair play though, he is a good teacher,' Gramp continued; 'very
particular and he will insist upon the purest form of the language. To tell the truth he has helped me out with some of
my poems.'

'Are there any swear words in Welsh?'

'Why do you want to know?'

Tim, already regretting his question, had been driven by
a curiosity derived from time spent in the office and the market where Welsh speaking had been universal but where
English had been the language of choice for profanities. 'I …
I was just wondering whether there was a word for something like "bugger" in Welsh.'

'For God's sake don't ask him that!'

'But when you say it no one seems to mind.'

'Because it is in English and it means bugger all in this
community; but not to him. He will take it literally.'… Gramp
paused and winked at him …'English always was the best
language for swearing.' …

Tim knew that there would be no further explanation.
The waters of difference between the two languages, when it
came to expletives, had intrigued him but would remain
muddy. …

The mist in the valley had risen to engulf them. Gramp
turned to go. 'Come on, Tim. Mari has our own roast beef and
God knows how many vegetables waiting. She likes to spoil
you when you are here on Sundays. … Then you must get
down to your books.'

# CHAPTER 7

**B**oz stood in front of his bathroom mirror inspecting the redness of his eyes and the untypical pallor of his complexion. He ran his fingers through his dark hair. Grey tufts were there; more of them. He bent down to the basin and splashed his face with cold water; then wiped it with a towel. A night out in the Legion was not a good preparation for today of all days. ... He peered out of the window into the darkness before dawn, groaned and shook his head. A sale of live and dead stock at the beginning of February was a rare event; a disaster – inevitably occasioned by some catastrophe for the vendors who, given the opportunity, would have chosen the traditional and more inviting seasons of spring or autumn. Boz dipped his shaving brush into the small bowl of hot water beside the basin; then rubbed it in the soap to make a lather. ... Apart from the time of year there would be other problems to contend with. He had been up there the week before. The farmer's wife and one of the daughters had been in tears, begging him to get there early; so the worst could be expected. It was hard on the women. They would need some comforting. ... That's where Tim would come in; that and filling in wherever the need arose. Boz applied the lather to his face and picked up his safety razor. There was something about Tim. ... Look how he'd liberated Teg from that pile of French letters. ... The girls in reception were always on about him, wiping fluff off his jacket, mothering him generally but he didn't seem to notice. Boz chuckled, put his razor down and picked up his toothbrush. ...

Catrin lay fast asleep. Rhodri and Elin were curled up in the crooks of her arms. They must have crept in while he was in the bathroom – the little monkeys. Boz stood for a moment, observing his family cuddled into the space of a few, warm square feet; safe against the cold. He smiled. If that bullet had been an inch to the left he would not have been here. His name would be on the plaque in the square and that would be that; Catrin with another man; no Rhodri and no Elin to brighten the world. Elin stirred, raised her head and blinked at him. Boz put his finger to his lips and she lay down again. Catrin had been displeased with his noisy return at midnight and now was not the time to wake her. He blew a kiss and left. ...

The back of Boz's Land Rover was uncomfortable, its canvas cover flapping in a freezing wind. Tim was sitting next to Teg. Facing them, in the half light of dawn, two craggy-faced drovers from the cattle market sat hunched over their sticks sharing a roll-up. Teg had introduced them as Ianto and Willy but no one had spoken since. Tim looked to the front. Dai was crammed into the relative comfort of the nearside passenger seat, the contortion of his back projecting his balding head forward. Between him and Boz was squeezed the diminutive figure of Miss Morgan, her account books and a heavy calculating machine clutched firmly to her knees. Tim had barely spoken with her. ... Avoiding unnecessary conversation and keeping mostly to her room she was regarded with awe by upper and lower orders of the office hierarchy.

There was nothing, it seemed, that she could not balance. Even the most chaotic presentations of figures came into line under her gaze. Referred to universally as 'Miss Morgan' she had become the undisputed mistress of her small but vital department of two girls and a dim lad. ...

The Land Rover went over a pothole, its full force felt through the steel bench seats. The drovers protested in Welsh and Boz replied in English. 'Sorry boys! You wait till we get to the driveway. It's bloody terrible.' One of the drovers picked up an old coil of rope which lay between them and sniffed at it with his large and pock-marked nose. 'Boz! There's a horrible smell in here,' he shouted, winking at Tim.

'It's my dog,' Boz riposted. 'Every time I take him out with the gun he rolls in cachi.'

'What's cachi?' Tim asked, immediately wishing he hadn't. Miss Morgan was shifting uneasily and the drover leaned towards him. 'Shit,' he whispered; 'it means shit.' Tim sat up, feeling his face reddening.

'It is not a very polite expression, Mr Tim,' said Teg. 'I don't suppose you are learning words like that with the Reverend Ebenezer.'

'Oh no; far from it,' said Tim, eager to escape his embarrassment. 'He's got me comparing Welsh and English translations of the Bible a lot of the time.'

'Oh dear,' Teg sighed. 'He's a devil for the Bible. ... I hope, at least, that it's the New Testament. The Old One seems so aggressive. ... I can see you may need bringing up to date. I can help you if you like.'

'I'd really appreciate that.'

'You may depend on me, Mr Tim; but you should stay with the Reverend Ebenezer,' said Teg with a misty, far-off look. 'He's wonderful at Eisteddfodau' …

Having survived the battering of the long driveway Miss Morgan and her books remained in the Land Rover, sheltered from a bitter, finger-biting wind with dampness on its breath. The rest of them stood on a farmyard which did not look as it should. Neglected piles of dung, rubbish and the rusting hulks of antique farm machinery lay scattered about in disorderly fashion. Without a word Boz had gone to the farmhouse on the far side of a range of decaying sheds to announce their arrival.

'Where the bloody hell are they?' muttered one of the drovers, looking at Tim as if for instruction.

'They?'

'The cattle,' came the sharp reply.

'Boz will find out soon enough,' said Dai, handing Tim a long stick with a fork at the top. 'I thought you might need this, Mr Tim. Thum-sticks are very useful at farm sales. You can keep it if you like.'

'I should have brought one of my own.'

'How could you know, Mr Tim? It is your first time, is it not?'

'Yes, … but …'

'You keep it. I make them in my spare time; find them in the woods; special ones sometimes. There are plenty more where that one came from.'

'You're a lucky young bugger,' cried the drover; 'famous he is – for sticking; won prizes in England and all!'

Tim's thumb rested comfortably in the polished cleft prepared for it. The stick seemed made for him; the right length,
slender and strong. 'Thank you, Dai', said Tim; 'you're very
kind.' He felt that his acceptance had been no match for the
challenge of the man's thoughtfulness and generosity. He
looked up, wanting to say more. Dai was still smiling but
there was something about him, hard to define; a weariness,
a subtraction ...

'Tim!' Boz was at his side. 'Come with me; and you Teg.
... It's a bloody shambles!' Boz took them to the far side of
the sheds and stopped. ... 'Look over there, will you.' Boz was
pointing at a gaunt and lanky man standing on the pathway
close to the farmhouse door. In front of him was a bentwood
chair upon which stood a bowl. Half of his face was covered
in thick shaving cream. He held a cut-throat razor in one hand
and a broken shard of mirror in the other. ...

'Who is he?' asked Tim, thinking that this looked more
like a comedy than a tragedy.

'He's our client. Hit the bottle before dawn by the look of
him! What a case! He's done bugger all. The cattle are out on
the land – somewhere – in February I ask you. The sheep are
all over the place. Nothing prepared and we're selling in a
couple of hours!'

'Perhaps I could have a word with him; remind him of his
obligations,' suggested Teg.

'Waste of time,' Boz muttered. 'The best thing would be
for you and Tim to see if the women are OK with the food
and everything. The Mrs is in a hell of a state; ... and get Miss
Morgan settled in the parlour with her books. Make sure they
light the fire there; then join me on the yard as soon as pos-

sible.'

Tim was feeling apprehensive. 'How do we get past him?'

'With difficulty,' replied Boz, turning to go; 'but don't let him delay you; and make sure the women are alright.'

In the event Tim, carrying the calculating machine, Teg, holding the account books and Miss Morgan, carrying a brief-case, had slipped past the man unchallenged, picking up the scent of stale whisky as they went. ...

'It is a shame,' Teg whispered, 'seeing him come to this. It's the bank, you see, that's pushed him over; but, to tell the truth, he was born in a dry summer.'.

Inside was pandemonium. Two young, red-faced girls in aprons were busy over an ancient stove. Two women were washing pots noisily in a deep sink at the back of the room. An older woman, her greying hair up in a bun and her eyes wet with tears, got up from a table and grasped Teg by the hands. He was speaking to her quietly, gently leading her back to the table; persuading her to sit down. One of the girls brought her a cup of tea; then another for Teg. Tim noticed that she, too, had been crying. The comforting drone of Teg's counsel was continuing, not a word of which Tim under-stood. He stood apart with Miss Morgan, practically unno-ticed; an uncomfortable observer of a scene he could only guess at. Suddenly the woman looked up at him, speaking in English. 'I am filled with shame – him not preparing. We begged him to get the cattle and the sheep. He got the cattle in yesterday evening but they escaped in the night. ... He left the gate to the shed open so what was the use?' The woman paused, rubbing her eyes. 'He was not always like this. It is not all his fault. Today, of all days though, he has abandoned us for the bottle. The shame of it! No one will come to the sale. They will know we are gone to the dogs. We shall be ruined!' She buried her head in her hands and started to wail. The two women stopped washing their pots, came across to the table and sat down either side of her. One put an arm around her. Tim's mind was a blank. He had suddenly been offered a speaking part in a family drama he knew nothing about; whose first language he did not share. He knew he would have to find words to arrest a further descent into despair. ... 'Please don't worry,' he blurted; ... 'we'll get the animals in. We' ve got a good team out there and I'm sure people will come to support you.' Tim hesitated, wondering whether to continue in the stunned silence he had created; ... 'and you shouldn't feel ashamed; you really shouldn't. This could happen to anybody. ... I'm sure that your husband has been under great strain. It's a time when neighbours should gather round and support you and I feel certain they will.'

There was a pause. The woman looked up, studying him for what seemed a long time. Then a half smile. 'You have a kind face and you have been a great comfort to me. I know that you will do your best for us.' Tim's inward sigh of relief was echoed in the room as the tension eased. One of the girls brought cups of tea for himself and Miss Morgan. She looked up at Tim. 'I put sugar in; you want sugar?'

'I don't think I've got time. We've got so much to do,' muttered Tim, wondering how, on earth, his promises could be made real.

'Will we see you at the lunch then?'

'Yes, you will.' ... Tim thought for a moment. 'Have you got a parlour?'

'Yes,' said the girl, looking puzzled ... 'and I've lit a fire there.'

'Good; ... then could you help Miss Morgan set up.' He turned to Miss Morgan. 'What do you need?'

'A table and two chairs,' she intoned; 'for a sale like this I can deal with the buyers one at a time.'

'Good;' Tim turned to the girl who was eying him with some admiration. 'Can you do that?'

'Yes I can; ... and thank you for being so good with my mother.' Blushing, she touched his sleeve and whispered. 'You have a lovely voice.'..

'Mr Tim!' Teg was at the door, beckoning.

Outside the 'client' had finished his shaving and was sprawled untidily upon a wooden bench, his back against the front wall of the house and humming to himself. His dark eyes had a brooding, unfocussed look about them and Tim noticed that he had cut himself, a rivulet of blood drying on his cheek.

'It's a mercy that he didn't cut his throat with that thing,' ventured Teg as they made their way around the sheds. ... 'Oh, my goodness!' he exclaimed, stopping. 'We didn't arrange a room for Miss Morgan.'

'Don't worry; it's done.'

Teg sighed with relief. 'If you don't mind me saying, Mr Tim, I thought, all in all, you did very well in there. They like you; trust you, you see.'

'I made a lot of promises.'

'Well, we'll just have to make sure that they are kept.'

How cattle could be caught in time; how neighbours

could be coerced into coming to the sale, Tim did not know but the events in the house had left him feeling confident; empowered; determined to do his best. Out on the yard things had already changed. Rubbish had been cleared; some of the machinery had been moved and temporary fencing marked the sale ring with entrance and exit points to and from the buildings. Boz was at the centre of operations, looking every inch the officer in his tweed cap, camouflage jacket, gaiters and boots. Around his neck hung a pair of khaki binoculars and a whistle. He was beckoning to the drovers, his voice raised. 'Come on boys; we've got to go!' He turned to Tim. 'Good; … just in time. How was it?'

'OK.'

Boz seemed not to want further explanation. The drovers and Dai had joined them. Boz was pointing at a dilapidated wood and corrugated iron building to the left. 'Willy, is that your holding shed?'

'Yes.'

'Is it secure?'

'As much as I can make it – like a silk purse out of a sow's ear.'

'Good; … then we'll drive them in the back when we can find the buggers. They're all bullocks and I've no doubt they're as wild as hawks on this place. The good news is that I've got a neighbour coming with a dog to get the sheep but he'll need Ianto and Willy to help him after we've penned the cattle. That means that Tim and Dai will have to wash the bullocks and do the ear and lot numbers on their own with Teg recording; sorry boys and I don't even know whether there's a hose in this bloody mess. Boz paused, shaking his head;

then continued, his voice clear and commanding, 'and Teg, while we're gone will you check that the ring is OK and choose a place for us to sell from; the rest of you come with me.' Boz led the way into an adjacent field where the ground rose away from them steeply. He stopped and pointed. … 'I reckon we'll see where they are from up there. Come on boys; quick as we can.'

'Yes … Sir,' Tim cried.

'We're not in the army now Tim,' said Boz, winking at him. …

But it felt like it; a section of men, properly led, their orders clear; heading out on a mission over a battlefield of rough pasture, closely cropped, frosted and oozing with liquid mud which sucked and squirted at them as they moved swiftly up-hill. … Tim had done well in the CCF at School, rising to the rank of colour-sergeant. His ally and his guiding light had been the retired sergeant-major who had seen plenty of action and who was stationed, oddly, in the crypt beneath School Chapel together with a substantial armoury of aged rifles, bren guns, blanks and dummy grenades. Tim had even thought of joining the regular army after leaving school but Mother had begged him not to …

'Get down; get down!' … They had reached the top of the hill. Boz was crouching close to the ground – gesturing them down; peering through his binoculars. He beckoned and Tim came up beside him, his breath misting in the icy stillness.

'There they are,' Boz whispered, as he handed over the binoculars. 'They've found the wettest place on the farm and that takes some doing here.' Tim studied the scene. They were there alright; up to their fetlocks; wallowing in a pool of mud and green slime formed in the low ground where two hedges met. He could literally see the whites of their eyes; wild, undisciplined eyes …

'What are you grinning about?'asked Boz, as he reached for the binoculars.

'Their eyes; … a bit like their owner's.'

'The bloody bank owns them,' said Boz, turning to the others. … 'Now this is what we do, boys. … Willy – you and I will go down behind them. Ianto, Tim and Dai – you work your way back downhill, keeping in the dead ground; then line out well back from the hedge. You'll need to cover it all the way to the yard if we're to stop the buggers breaking out. … Now, for God's sake, don't let them see you before the whistle or they won't just be on the next farm; they'll be in the next parish!'


Half an hour later the cattle had been chased into a tin shed and the washing had begun. Tim had been put in charge of the hose but the flow from that was so inadequate that they decided to fill buckets instead. Tim had to throw buckets of water over each animal while Dai laboured at their filthy hides with a yard brush. They had done ten when he stopped and leaned upon his brush handle, breathing heavily. …

'Dai, let me do the scrubbing for a while,' said Tim.

'No, Mr Tim; I have done this many times and you will get very dirty.'

'I don't mind. I've got a waterproof and leggings.'

'Perhaps another time, Mr Tim; when the beasts are not so wild and filthy.' He leaned forward and patted one on its flank. 'They're not in bad condition though, for February, all things considered. ... We had better get on; another twenty five to do.'

After the washing, which Dai had declared was anything but perfect, there was only an hour to go before the start of the sale. A few people were beginning to arrive and wander about. A primus stove was fetched from the Land Rover and a metal pot of what looked like solidified toffee was set over its blue flame. Upon inquiry Tim was told that this was gum made from bones and hooves. In a molten state nothing stuck like it. If you got it on your clothes it was a waste of time trying to get it off. ... Teg joined them with his sale sheets, standing well clear. Tim, due to his height, was appointed reader of ear numbers. The job did not turn out to be as easy as it sounded. Dai would corner a beast and compress it against railings while Tim would grab an ear, turn it inside out and, with the aid of a torch, attempt to read the number tattooed inside. The twilight in the shed and the steam coming off the resentful animals made matters worse. The beasts proved reluctant; shifting, snorting and stamping. One of them trod on his foot but he didn't say anything. When his companion went to the primus stove to apply a gobbet of glue to a numbered label with the firm's name around the outside, a big bullock, its steaming breath and its bulging eyes the acme of hostility, pushed Tim against a rail. ... They finished with ten minutes to spare. The pervasive smell of cattle and boiling glue continued to cling but Tim was feeling pleased with himself. Dai came out of the shed to join him. 'I hope I didn't hold you up in there,' said Tim, apologetically.

'If you should ask me, Mr Tim, I think you did very well. Those beasts have probably been out all winter.'

'They didn't like us, did they?'

'Not surprising really; being chased out of their familiar field into a dark shed; buckets of water over them and ears being turned inside out.'

Tim laughed out loud. He was beginning to feel easy in this man's company. He looked about him. 'There's a good crowd here.'

'Yes, Mr Tim; not bad at all and I can see there are some butchers here too. We may be able to do well enough for them. ... I do hope so.'

Silence engulfed them both as they observed the crowd gathering around the sale ring, vying for places at the front, gossiping, laughing, joking with one another in voices raised against the totality of sound. A cart had been placed in a prominent position for Boz to sell from and Teg to clerk. Tim knew that the combination of those two, who, between them, would know almost everybody present, offered the best that the firm could give to their beleaguered clients and he felt proud to be part of what was, undoubtedly, a rescue operation. He glanced at Dai who seemed lost in thought. Today could be bringing some bad memories. ... A neat looking man with thinning, silver hair and wearing a black suit was standing near the cart in close conversation with Teg. 'Who's with Teg?' asked Tim, breaking the silence which he felt was becoming too heavy.

'That is the Minister of Bethesda, Mr Tim. ... Good of him to come what with the drinking and all but he will be here for the wife; and to keep the second book.'

'What's that?'

'Essential at any farm sale, Mr Tim. It is a separate record of what was sold, who the buyers were and how much they paid so the family can see afterwards what support they got from their friends and neighbours. ... You see the auctioneers will only let them have the figures and the money; but not the names.'

'What if a neighbour doesn't come and buy?'

'Not good, Mr Tim. It would be remembered against him; talked about; and, if he was ever to have a sale of his own, he may not have all the support he might want. That is why neighbours and friends are keen to get their names on the book ... and at tidy prices.'

The bar of the Tafarn Bach looked like the front parlour of any farmhouse, the only indication of its commercial activity being a square hole in its back wall through which jugs of ale could be passed. Old oak chairs were scattered about a couple of tables around a fireplace. A chaise longue stood against the front wall, looking strangely out of place, its faded blue cover torn at a corner with the stuffing coming out. The walls were a livid, smoke-stained green and unadorned with the exception of a picture of a large, brown bull and a sampler urging its readers to "Praise God Always." Tim was trying to read its date. ...

'Are you praising God, Tim?' Boz shouted from the hatchway.

'I'm praising this beer,' replied Tim cheerfully, turning towards his companions and raising his tankard; pleased that he had found an amusing riposte which had made them laugh.

'Well, we might as well praise God boys,' said Boz, finishing his pint. 'Today was a bloody miracle! Well done all of you. I never saw such prices and some of the stuff they were buying was almost worthless!'

'Even the butchers and the dealers were more generous than usual,' chirruped Teg. 'I spoke with some of them before the sale; told them the problem. ... I think they took pity.'

'Then you did a bloody good job, Teg,' said Boz, 'and, as for the neighbours, they rescued that family. ... It makes me proud to be Welsh. That poor woman was in a terrible state and, in all fairness, for an Englishman, you did a hell of a job on her, Tim. She thinks the world of you, I can tell you; and she gave you a hug at the end; and the daughters!' There was laughter as Boz brought the jug from the table and topped up Tim's tankard. He returned to the hole in the wall and shouted 'Un bach to, Maggie.'

'We must get this money into the bank,' piped Miss Morgan, who had remained silent, perched on a wooden bench against the back wall. She was pointing at the briefcase beside her. 'We mustn't be long now. It's not right – with all this money!'

Miss Morgan had been brought to the Tafarn, protesting all the way; considering the place not respectable enough for single women or any woman for that matter. Maggie, the publican who, according to Boz, had a relaxed attitude to licensing hours, had opened early for them and had done her best to be welcoming; poking at the dull glow of the fire. An extensive search of the premises had led to the discovery of a dust-covered bottle of sweet sherry, half its contents gone and of uncertain date. Boz had poured a schooner for Miss Morgan and, although she had protested at the amount, Tim could see that her glass was already empty. Boz had collected the new jug and was moving among the company, refilling the variety of pottery tankards for which the place was apparently famed. He grabbed Miss Morgan's glass and went to the hole in the wall, demanding a refill.

'Only if you come with me to the bank and see me put the pouches in the night safe,' she cried, wagging her finger at him.

'I will drive you to the bank and we'll all see you do it,' replied Boz, with a grin.

'Very well then; just the one,' said Miss Morgan, visibly relieved of her solo responsibility; 'and not too much this time.'

'I have to say, Miss Morgan,' declared Boz, 'that you excelled yourself today. Your announcement of the result could not have come at a better moment; … just in time to rescue the man of God from our client. …'

The men were doubling up with laughter and Tim was joining in; reflecting upon the dramatic events at the lunch laid on by the women at the end of the sale. Boz had parked him next to the Minister which had been fairly hard going. They had found common ground over The Reverend Ebenezer and the necessity to learn Welsh which had led on to how much he had learned already. He had been rescued from this disagreeable situation when the 'client' had come in by the front door, breathing heavily, smelling of spirits and covered in mud. He had promptly grasped the Minister's neat hands and knelt, fixing him with wild eyes, words pouring out – all in Welsh and wouldn't let go in spite of the Minister's polite efforts to free himself from the vice-like grip. The proceedings were brought to an abrupt halt by the triumphal entrance of Miss Morgan, holding a paper. She had waited for silence; then, half smiling, she had delivered the figures in a pure, childlike voice as might an angel holding the key to the household's future. Pandemonium had followed with, as far as Tim could tell, the client praising God and his wife praising her neighbours.

On the way to the Tafarn Bach Teg had translated the man's outpourings. He had spent the time of the sale aimlessly wandering the farm looking for his livestock. At the top of the hill he had, apparently, been brought to his senses by a direct and very firm message from The Lord to repent of his misdoings and make amends, or else. This he was, apparently, determined to do forthwith. 'I hope he sticks by that,' muttered Teg, 'but the call of the bottle, when it gets a hold on you, is very powerful. ... Did you see him with whisky at the end, trying to share it round? The Minister took the bottle off him before he had opened it, thanks be to God. It was not fitting that we should stay there for any kind of celebration. We would be putting temptation in his way.' Teg had paused thoughtfully and sighed. 'We can only hope and pray that his is a true repentance – for the sake of his family.' ...

Miss Morgan accepted Boz's compliment with a demure satisfaction and a broad smile; a rarity by all accounts and a sign that the sherry was doing its work. Conversation was winging effortlessly from Welsh to English and back again and Tim was conscious of an intention not to exclude him. He had noticed before, though, a tendency to wander freely between the two languages, particularly in matters of a technical or commercial nature. ... He took another mouthful of the beer which, according to Boz, was stored in a cool cave within the rock face against which the place was built. He peered into his tankard. The ale was remarkably clear; amber-coloured with the sweetness of malt and the sharpness of hops. ... He would have to persuade Rhyd and James to come up here in their Easter Vac. ... A door to the right of the hole in the wall opened and the publican entered, carrying a bucket of coals. She moved to the fireplace and added some to its dying glow, poked the result and straightened up. She was not what Tim had expected. Tall, large-breasted with long, black hair hanging over her shoulders and the swarthy, bohemian complexion of a traveller, her movements were fluid; almost elegant. She looked him up and down, her dark eyes beckoning. Tim returned her gaze momentarily, imagining that she must have been beautiful once. She spoke to him in Welsh, her voice rich and deep and Tim guessed that this was a greeting. ... 'Nos da,' he replied, unable to think of anything else. She nodded at him in a puzzled way.

Boz intervened. '"Nos Da" is like saying "Goodbye" after dark, Tim. You're not leaving us are you?' The drovers were laughing again but the woman had already lost interest in him and had turned her attention to Miss Morgan curious, may'be, to know the only other woman on her premises in the company of men. Miss Morgan sat, staring up at her hostess, with a look normally reserved for a snake by a mongoose and clutching her briefcase to her diminutive bosom.

Dai, who was sitting next to Tim, had been silent for some time, staring into the fire. 'Will the total be enough to get them out of trouble?' Tim asked, anxious to make conversation.

The reply was slow in coming. 'The neighbours tell me that they should be able to pay the bank off and finish the bungalow they were building for their retirement but, in truth, that was their undoing. ... He borrowed and spent far too much on it and he's only a tenant of his farm; ... but who am I to say that?' Dai paused, his eyes cast downwards, stooping to sip at his beer. 'Something like this happened to me years ago, Mr Tim; and I got my farm from my father. I knew every inch of it from the time I was a small child running free in its fields; felt its soil in my hands, walked it every day, cared for it, loved it like a woman; the fields and the woods changing with the seasons; always renewing itself. ... It had become part of me.' ... He touched his shoulder. 'I sometimes wonder whether this affliction is my punishment for losing it.' Tim couldn't find words which would match the weight of the man's grief. ... 'I should be thankful, though,' Dai continued, 'to have a job which keeps me in touch with my old neighbours and friends who care about me. ... I know everybody here, Mr Tim and have been shown nothing but kindness; and that is the greatest of blessings.'

Half an hour later they were standing outside. A half moon, low in the sky, was lighting up the leafless tops and skeletal branches of the trees on the far side of the valley. ... Tim took a deep breath. A drift of freezing air, blowing up the cwm, carried with it the smell of dead leaves and decaying wood but also a certain freshness; a life giving winter sharpness burning in the nostrils; hinting at spring.

'Come on, Tim!' Boz was calling from the Land Rover, ready to go.

# CHAPTER 8

The Brig seemed to be in a good mood. 'Today's adventure is your idea, Barrington-Lewis; so I shall expect it to be worthwhile. ... You spoke to the widow?'

'Yes sir; over the telephone. She says the field's partly under water.'

'She's probably making a fuss about nothing; just like her late husband; a crafty fellow; had to look out for him – always wanting us to spend more money. ... The Estate has entrusted me with its purse strings,' he continued, wiping condensation off the windscreen with his handkerchief, 'and, thanks to the tax man, there's practically damn all in the purse. ...You have to keep a constant qui-vive on these people. They're always out for what they can get in the way of unnecessary improvements so you'll have to impress me; you understand?'

'Yes sir.'

'You're not letting sentimentality get the better of you, are you?'

'No sir; but she's taken on the tenancy and we should, at least, take a look.'

The Brig changed gear, the shocking, metallic crunch of its box and the whine of its puny engine signifying to Tim that the Ford Popular was, at least, democratic in its dislike of its drivers. 'Are you thinking of changing the car sir?'

'Of course not,' the Brig snapped; 'and don't be impertinent. There's plenty of life in her yet as long as you don't drive her too fast and have some respect for the gear box.'...

They had reached the top of a hill and the Brig pulled into a lay-by. Heavy rain overnight had brought a sparkling clarity to the morning. From where they had parked they could look down into a broad valley of neat fields and woods, the lower land already exchanging its winter browns for emerald growth. Trees in the woodland on the far side had become a haze of light greens – luminous; dappled by sunshine and the passage of clouds. ...

'April tomorrow,' said the Brig, 'and the river's quite full.' Tim could trace its brown, circuitous course dividing the valley floor in the manner of a jigsaw. Some water had escaped its banks to lie in pools; bright surfaces reflecting the sky or rippled by the breeze. A small stone bridge formed a crossing close to a junction of two lanes. ...

'Where's the farm plan?' asked the Brig. Tim handed him the scroll he had, at the last minute, remembered to collect from the Drawing Office. 'Good,' continued the Brig. 'This is what we do. I'll walk down to the farmhouse from here; opportunity to inspect the land; could be in a hell of a state what with the man dying and a change of tenancy. You drive on downhill and take the track on the left just before the bridge. It's quite rough so you be damned careful with my car, whatever you may think of it! What time does your watch say?'

'Twenty past ten, sir.'

'We'll synchronise on that. I'll meet you on the yard at eleven hundred hours; right?'

'Yes sir; but what do I do while I'm waiting?'

'What do you think, boy? Make yourself known to the lady; tell her I'm on my way down; ... an opportunity, may'be, for you to practice your Welsh though God only knows why you're bothering to learn it; and remember – you are not to make any promises whatsoever about whatever she's rabbiting on about.'

'Very well, sir.'

The Brig furled the map, reached for his shepherd's crook, unwound himself from the car and made off downhill. ...

As he nursed the car along a driveway full of potholes filled with muddy water Tim decided that he would, at least, greet the lady in Welsh. Their telephone conversation had been awkward and stilted and, of necessity, in English. He had managed to establish some rules of grammar and pronunciation with The Reverend Ebenezer and had gleaned some useful expressions from Teg. Provided he could stick with subjects like the weather it should be OK. He turned into a farmyard surrounded by stone buildings and tin sheds. At the top end stood the farmhouse – white-painted, its small windows divided into many panes and traditionally spaced left and right of its front door. In front a small forecourt was enclosed by a low stone wall with a flight of steps down to the yard. Tim, with his new-found ability to examine buildings for faults, noted that some slates had slipped around the chimney stacks at either end. The door opened and a woman, in dungarees and wellington boots, came down the steps to meet him. She was taller than he expected and difficult to age, with a wind-tanned complexion and close-cropped, brown hair – turning to silver. ... Tim decided to open with 'Bore Da' (good morning). He had pre-planned a sentence which would explain that the Brig was making his way down to them and he also had several comments about the rain up his sleeve and the fact that he was learning Welsh. If he played his cards right he wouldn't run out of the language before the Brig came to the rescue. ... In the event his preparation proved a waste of time. It seemed that his pronunciation, carefully monitored by The Reverend Ebenezer, had been good enough to fool her into thinking he was fluent. She was off like a long-dog, launching into a waterfall of gabbled words; an undecipherable litany, rising and falling and which seemed to have no end. It appeared that she was unburdening herself of something but her weathered features made her emotions hard to define. May'be she was on about the flooding and he needed to be careful. In the rare gaps between her outpourings he decided that nodding and smiling would suffice. Increasingly anxious not to get trapped into some kind of promise to pay for improvements he finally managed to suggest, in broken Welsh, that she was, no doubt, enjoying the challenge of running the farm and that, with the coming of April, the weather would soon improve. ... It was then that he noticed a change in her demeanour. She was slowing down, her dark eyes widening, looking wary and she was backing away from him. Tim was never so happy to see the Brig. So was she, it seemed – trotting across the yard to him as if to seek his protection. Now they were in a conversation which, in the chill wind, he could not hear. The Brig looked towards him and shook his head. ...

The tenant led them to a field, the lowest third of which was under water. 'What do you do next?' asked the Brig, handing Tim the plan.

'Mark the extent of the flooding, sir.'

'And then what?'

'I don't know, sir.'

'How about asking Mrs ... here – the tenant some questions about it?'

'There's water here from November to May,' bleated the lady, cutting in before Tim could speak; 'only dries out in the summer and then it's too soft for the cattle; not good for sheep either and there are rushes everywhere. ... I could turn it into good pasture and ...'

'Well, Barrington-Lewis,' said the Brig, interrupting. 'Where do you think it's coming from?'

'The water, sir?'

'What else?'

'I'm not really sure sir. Is it a high water table?'

'If it was then the whole damn lot of the lower ground would be inundated. Have a look there.' The Brig was pointing at a disturbance; a welling up of water in front of them. 'What do you think that is?'

'It looks like a spring.'

'Yes; and a damn strong one at that. There are probably a number of them here. You have to think of the geography. Look up there;' the Brig was pointing up the hill Tim had driven down. 'That high ground's full of rain at this time of year and the stuff's obeying gravity and looking for a way out – so, as soon as it levels out, it finds the weak spots in the geology and surfaces; and the hedges we're looking at are acting as a dam.'

An idea was forming in Tim's mind. 'There may be a solution, sir.'

'We don't discuss solutions now,' snapped the Brig; 'you've marked the plan?'

'Yes sir,'

'Good; how many acres do you think are involved?'

Tim consulted his plan. 'The whole field's six acres, sir; ... I would say two.'

'That's about right,' said the Brig, looking at his watch; 'time to go.'

When they returned to the yard the tenant offered them tea and Welsh cakes which she declared had been baked that morning but the Brig declined upon the excuse of another appointment. They were bidding farewell when the Brig, apparently concerned not to leave her with the impression that he did not care about her new circumstances, enquired as to where her husband was buried. ...

'Over there,' sighed the lady, pointing to the far side of the valley where a small, grey chapel stood, its compact graveyard clinging to the hillside. 'He's got a wonderful stone,' she continued, her eyes moistening; 'in grey marble with a lovely cherub on top ... and gold writing.'

'Good,' said the Brig, breezily, following her gaze; 'he should be able to keep an eye on you from there.'

As they drove slowly uphill Tim concluded that the Brig, hardened, no doubt, by his military experience, regarded death as an ordinary affair; merely a natural consequence of living. At the top of the hill the Brig pulled into the same lay-by and burrowed into his jacket pocket. 'Time for our pieces; am I supposed to feed you?'

'No thank you, sir,' said Tim, quickly reaching for the tin with the hinged lid he had placed on the floor of the car.

'Do you make your own?' asked the Brig, biting into a damp sandwich.

'My landlady does a packed lunch for me every day.'

'Then you should consider yourself spoilt.' Tim opened the lid. Inside were the familiar sandwiches of cheese, ham, farm butter and home baked bread, its fresh smell making his mouth water; also a hard boiled egg and an apple. ...

'Now, Barrington-Lewis, I've a bone to pick with you,' said the Brig, offering Tim the remains of his flask of warm coffee in a bent cup. 'If you will insist upon learning this damned tricky language I don't expect you to go round the county scaring people out of their wits in the firm's time.'

'I'm sorry sir,' muttered Tim, not knowing exactly what he was supposed to be sorry about. He looked at the Brig whose eyes were fixed upon him and thought he detected amusement among the wrinkles.

'She thought you were insane; that you'd been let out of a lunatic asylum for the day. ... If it's any comfort to you I did take the trouble to explain that, as far as I knew, you were not stark mad and that you were trying to learn the language; but I think she's still pretty wary of you.'

'What did I do, sir?' asked Tim, biting his lip.

'Well, apparently, she was giving you a blow by blow account of the funeral and the burial of her late husband and all you could do, it seems, was to comment upon the weather and suggest that she must be enjoying herself.'

'Oh God. ... How shall I make it up to her?'

'Don't bother; just don't try your Welsh on her again; she's in an edgy state; besides which they make a hell of a song and a dance about death around here. ... I had to go to one of their damned funerals once; of some tenant whose family insisted on my being there. .... I thought it would never end. Ten, I ask you, no less than ten Ministers went into bat! I couldn't understand a bloody word although God knows what they could find to say about him. I could have done his eulogy in thirty seconds. ... The man was an out and out knave; would have sold his own mother at the right price!' Tim laughed, wondering whether the Brig's marathon had been in Jabez Chapel but decided not to ask. ...

The Popular was blessedly quiet, freewheeling downhill. The Brig had explained that, whereas petrol was necessary to get up a hill, it was patently ridiculous to use the stuff on the way down. 'Was Boz an officer in the War, sir?' asked Tim, wanting to steer the conversation away from any further examination of his faux pas.

'Yes, he was; and I wish people would call him "Captain Thomas."'

'He doesn't seem to want that.'

'Well, he should. ... He's letting the side down; had a good record, so it seems.'

'What did he do, sir?'

'Served in Europe for the latter half of the war; and he got a military cross for rescuing not one but two wounded men in his company; under fire. He took a bullet getting the second man.'

'He never talks about it, sir.'

'The best ones don't,' muttered the Brig, crunching into a

lower gear to climb the next hill. ... 'The second man he recovered died of his wounds; the loss haunts him, I gather, although, God knows, he did well enough to save one.' The Brig paused. ... 'I gather your father was killed in action.'

'At the end of it,' mumbled Tim, regretting this further twist in the conversation. ... The Brig braked savagely, propelling Tim forward; then swerved to avoid a tractor. 'Such is war,' he continued, 'no time to bloody well think; things happening all over the place and, if you mope about the loss of your men too much, you're finished; a wreck. A lot of it's about luck; being in the wrong place at the wrong time. ... I remember a subaltern of mine; an excellent young officer; took a bullet in the head standing right next to me; dropped like a sack of potatoes – right at my feet. ... He was due to inherit a useful estate in Norfolk when he got home. All he ended up with was six foot by two in the Hindu Kush and he's still there as far as I know. Those tribesmen were crafty beggars; bloody accurate over long distance; barely heard the shot. ... Do you fish?'

'Yes,' said Tim, taken aback by the sudden change in the Brig's order of priorities but grateful to have left the war behind.

'Good; when the season gets going I'll give you a few day tickets to fish my water; excellent for sea-trout in July; fly only, mind you. I will not tolerate any damned spinners or worms! ... Now, to business; I want you to think carefully about what you've seen and heard. We've lost the best part of a day fiddling around out there so you'd better come back with something sensible.'

Tim reckoned he had come upon a good idea but he

wasn't going to risk telling the Brig without further investigation. 'Could I take some levels, sir, where the water is lying?'

'Good God, boy! Levels; you reckon you need levels.' The Brig thought for a moment. 'Very well; it's up to you. It might be good for your education but don't hang about too long out there and, remember – agree to nothing!'

The following morning Tim went to see Miss Morgan in accounts and enquired as to whether he could borrow Billy for a few hours to hold the levelling staff. She readily agreed to release him from his duties of fetching and carrying boxes and papers, tea and coffee, believing that such an experience might improve him. Billy had, it seemed, not been born with many advantages – short in stature, sallow and skinny with pale green eyes that had the look of one studying far horizons. By common consent, however, he possessed one remarkable ability – to conjure fish out of water in all weathers by fair means or foul. A lad of few words he was reputed to reserve them for trout, talking them onto his hook or into his net. If you wanted a fish when no one else had one, he was your man and he always kept tackle and a pair of waders in the office – ready to go down to the river after work. ....

By lunchtime they had returned from their outing. The dumpy level, borrowed from the drawing office, hadn't been too difficult to set up but Billy, wading in the flood water, had taken some persuasion to hold the staff upright and to stay still. The lady had offered tea and Welsh cakes again and Tim, believing that this might make up for his previous insults, had happily accepted. Billy, his half frozen legs warmed by her open fire, her hot tea with a dash of whisky and her encouragement had come into his own; blossoming suddenly into Welsh; speaking in a child-like voice but, at least, with some fluency. ... Tim took the results of his survey to the drawing office. There he set up a board and cartridge paper and began plotting in pencil. The level readings were telling him that there was a natural depression in the ground. He felt confident. It was time to put flesh on the bones of his idea. Remembering the guidance in his study papers he chose a scale of one quarter inch to the foot for the horizontal and one inch to the foot for the vertical in order to properly reflect and make readable the result of his levelling exercise.

Having made the required appointment Tim stood, drawing in hand, in front of the Brig. "Inca," having greeted him with the customary growl, had allowed Tim to pat him before settling back into his basket. 'Well,' said the Brig, looking up at him, 'what have you got there?'

'A solution I have come up with about the flooding, sir. I think you'll find it quite interesting.' There was something about the Brig's demeanour which Tim found unsettling. 'Would you like to see it, sir? ... I've shown it on this drawing to proper scales.'

'No; you tell me what's it's about first.'

'Well, sir; it seems that the real cause of the problem are the springs which you identified.'

'Good – so far,' cut in the Brig.

'Well, the levels I have taken suggest that, with further excavation of the deepest part and the creation of a curved embankment, we could, according to my calculations, contain water up to a depth of about five feet. If we also create a sluice and a ditch running down the hedge to the next field there is enough of a drop there to discharge excess water into an existing watercourse and so prevent overflow.' Tim looked up from his drawing, feeling pleased with his explanation but the Brig remained disturbingly silent and his features impassive. ... 'Such a reservoir,' he continued, 'could be very useful in a drought and the land beyond the embankment could be kept dry all the year round.'

The Brig reached for the drawing and scanned it briefly; then looked up, his face twisted into an attitude of disbelief, his eyes narrowing. 'So,' he barked, 'you're recommending that we build something like the bloody Aswan Dam, are you? You're suggesting that the farm is in the Egyptian desert rather than a place where it hardly ever stops pouring with bloody rain?' The Brig's tirade was allowing no room for answers. ... 'Have you,' he continued, 'thought what it would cost – this grand work of engineering?'

'No sir,' said Tim, looking down, fighting to conceal his bitter disappointment; 'the drawings are at a preliminary stage.'

'And that's where they'll stay,' shouted the Brig. 'You'd bankrupt the estate for the sake of a few soggy acres worth a fraction of the cost of what you're proposing.' The Brig paused to look at the plan again. 'I see you have them marked.'

'What, sir?'

'Trees; on the hedge? ...What are they?'

'Oak trees, sir,' said Tim, under his breath; 'hedgerow oaks and some alder.'

'Right – trees like that and water in the winter; plenty of

cover. What does that tell you?'

'I don't know, sir.'

'Ducks, boy, ducks! That's what it tells me. Perfect cover for em; with a little bit of feeding it'll be covered with the blighters for most of the winter.'

'But that wouldn't benefit the tenant,' said Tim, suddenly feeling angry, his face flushing; wanting to fight back. 'She needs the grazing and she is paying the rent.'

'Forget the tenant. You have to see the whole picture. As you should know from your papers, landlords are in the habit of reserving sporting rights which is certainly the case here. If we leave things as they are and don't spend a penny they'll have the benefit of a large duck pond in the season; of course the tenant gets the rough grazing in the summer as before and …'

'But that doesn't seem fair,' said Tim, cutting in, his voice raised, feeling that he would be part of an injustice.

'Life isn't fair, Barrington-Lewis; or haven't you noticed? … I can't see why you're worrying about her. We'll offer her a modest abatement in the rent to compensate; she'll probably end up better off.'


Tim found refuge in the drawing office. He sat at his desk feeling wretched, his eyes moistening, the Brig's rebuke still ringing in his ears. He looked at his drawing which had been such a waste of time and effort. It seemed that every small triumph was extinguished by a greater humiliation. He looked through the window. It was raining heavily outside and the drab wreck of Rhywle castle appeared more depressing than ever. He wanted to be anywhere but here. … He felt a tap on his shoulder and turned to face Boz. 'I've just had a bloody awful telling off by the Brig', he blurted, his defences down; 'I don't know whether I can go on with all this.'

'I did hear him laying into you,' said Boz.

'God,' said Tim, rubbing his eyes; 'the whole bloody office will have listened in.'

'They won't take any notice. He's so often like that they've got used to it. It's his way. He's an old war-horse but he's got a good heart under all that bluster.' ...

'Well, I can't see it,' said Tim, miserably.

Boz leaned over to look at the drawing. 'You've done a good job here, Tim, with colouring and lots of detail. ... What was his idea?'

'To leave the flooding alone and let the landlords use it for flighting duck,' said Tim despondently. 'It doesn't seem fair.'

Boz looked at the drawing again. 'I think he's got a point there, Tim. ... In his way he's probably trying to tell you that, on the ground, solutions are often simpler than the fancy stuff you're reading about for your examinations. When it comes to estate work he knows what it's all about – money largely or, more often than not, the lack of it. He could teach you a lot of practical stuff if you can put up with him; and don't worry about the tenant; he'll see her right; he won't be unfair. After all he did let her have the tenancy when her husband died.' ... Tim, beginning to recognise his lack of common sense, picked up the drawing. 'I think I should tear it up.'

'Don't,' said Boz. 'Keep it. You might be able to use it in one of your practical exams; could save you a lot of time later.

… Come on; it's lunchtime; let's go for a pint.'

'I don't think he has any time for me,' said Tim, as they turned to leave. 'He's always using my surname – both barrels. It seems so formal; and I've been working with him on and off for months.'

'That's the way he is. In his head he's still in the army and pre-war at that,' replied Boz, breezily, as they walked through reception; 'and be thankful he uses your surname however long it is. It's because he regards you as a subaltern in training. He'd only use your Christian name if he thought you were other ranks or the gardener or something; so take it as a compliment. …

The next day Tim was summoned to the Brig's office. In expectation of a further dressing down he was determined that, this time, he would look his adversary in the eye and give a good account of himself; but the Brig wasn't looking at him. He was making notes. When he had finished he sat back and said 'I've had a phone call from the wife of that machine-buff tenant of ours; … and it involves you.'

'In what way, sir?'

'She seems to have a high opinion of you, though God knows why?'

'But all my conversations were with her husband.'

'He's not there, apparently; away for a few days at one of those oil engine fairs up in England. A crank meeting a whole lot of other cranks I would imagine.'

'Has she said what it's about?'

'She's remarkably non-specific; rather an odd lady if you should ask me; a bit vacant-minded but she intimated that it may be about the boundary problem. ... Perhaps she wants to tell us something when her husband isn't around. It could turn out to be a delicate matter. If you feel you can't handle it I could, of course, go up there myself.' ...

'No sir,' said Tim hastily, his pulse quickening, 'I'll go.'

The Brig looked him up and down. 'Very well; but you are not, I repeat not to agree to any improvements whatsoever. This might just be a ploy on her part to get us to spend more money on the house.'

'When do I go, sir?'

'Now, of course; while her husband is away.'

'Did she ask for me particularly, sir?'

'She made it fairly clear that she would prefer to talk to you rather than anyone else.'

Tim was on the farmyard by ten o'clock. He had driven there like Jehu, urging the Minor along the narrow lanes, his mind a turmoil of curiosity and anticipation. His wish to see her again had been granted but in the strangest of ways. The whole thing could turn out to be a big disappointment – merely a conversation about trespass; another check on the fence across the brook. As he walked towards the house he concluded that his imagination had been running wild; that he should pull himself together and expect no more than tea and Welsh cakes. ...

Tim pulled into a lay-by and looked at his watch. It was half past twelve. He rolled down the window, reached for a cigarette and lit up. ... The door of the farmhouse had been open. He had heard her crying. He had called out. She had come into the hall, her beautiful eyes wet with tears. He had asked whether there was anything he could do. She had said nothing, coming to him, clasping him, laying her head upon his shoulder. He had held her tight, wanting to comfort her, patting her shoulder, hoping that her sobbing would cease. She had kissed his neck; then his cheek; then his lips and he had responded. He had followed her upstairs, her silken slacks and white blouse hinting at the slim, vulnerable beauty beneath. ... Her bedroom had been a place apart, its window concealed by voluminous, white curtains; the blue carpet deep-piled; the bed large with clean, inviting sheets. She had let down her hair; golden tresses covering her pale shoulders and drifting down her back. She had removed a teddy bear from the junction of pillows and placed it on an elegant, gilded chair. He could remember its accusing, button eyes observing him as he lay beside her. ... Hearing a noise in the yard he had sat up in panic, reaching for his clothes. She had put a finger to her lips and drawn him back, enfolding him in the warm and perfumed softness of herself. The dread, which had tightened his stomach and made his heart race, had been transformed into a compelling desire – careless and disorderly; driving him on. At the end she had sighed; a long exhalation which had lasted and lasted. ... There had been no conversation; hardly a word had passed between them and he didn't even know her name. He blushed at the thought. She had wept as he left her. He had asked whether he could see her again. She had said nothing – putting her slender hand to his lips and shaking her head. What was that supposed to mean? She had made it so easy for him but, perhaps, in his virginity, he had disappointed her. ...

From where he had parked he could look back at the place he had come from – the modest, whitewashed farmhouse and its attendant sheds, the course of the brook, the wet meadows either side; the sloping, pocket sized fields bright with the intensity of spring; the hill pasture above still clad in the browns of winter. He knew he had taken something; something important from a man with probably little to give – for this windswept place would be hard to work and turn to profit. ... His dreams had been turned into an unfamiliar reality – a battleground where guilt was being consumed by the fire she had kindled within him for he longed to see her again; to lie close; to be held in the scented paradise she had so briefly created for him.

# CHAPTER 9

Sophie darling, you look a picture,' cried Mother, standing back to admire her handiwork. 'I'm so glad I found that tulle; just right for a vestal virgin.'

'I look a complete frump,' retorted Sophie, examining herself in a mirror, gathering her long hair into a diamante clip; 'anyway, I don't want to be a vestal virgin!'

'But you agreed,' pleaded Mother. 'You and Camilla and Francesca were dressing up as a matching threesome.'

'I bet they look better than this; especially Cam,' muttered Sophie, tugging at the diaphanous extensions under her arms.

'Tim's not complaining,' Mother countered.

'Yes he is; but not to you, Mother. He reckons his toga's too short. He's really embarrassed. … Did Roman Senators show their knees?'

'Yes they did.'

'Who says?'

'The book I've bought. … Togas went up in the first century.'

'Did it have to be the first century?'

'If it had been earlier or later,' replied Mother, thoughtfully, 'I'd have had to use another sheet.'

'Poor Tim.'

'He'll love it. He's got a week's holiday ahead of him. His friends are home and I'm sure all you young things will have a whale of a time.'

'At the Distressed Gentlefolk's Fancy Dress Ball! ... The band has an average age of eighty and there's no alcohol!'

'Part of its charm, Sophie dear; one of the reasons why it's such an important event in the social calendar. ... Everybody behaves themselves so well; lots of civilised conversation – and dancing. ... Anyway, I'm looking forward to it,' continued Mother, making an adjustment to the shoulder strap of her green ball gown; 'and what a joy to be driven there by the Merit-Owens.' ... There was a knock on the bedroom door. 'Come in Tim,' cried Mother. ... 'Now I think that you look every inch the Roman; a proper Senator.' Sophie, putting her hand to her mouth, had started to snigger.

'I look a bit of an idiot,' muttered Tim, tugging at his toga; 'it's like a nappy; and I'm cold.'

'It won't be cold there, Tim dear, with all those people; and Sir Harry always has log fires. ... You can take a rug if you like.'

'What can I do with that, Mother?'

'Wrap it round your shoulders if you need to.'

'I'll look like a beggar.'

'Damn it,' Sophie exclaimed, looking in the mirror; 'you've made my mascara run, Tim.'

'It's not my fault.'

'Yes it is – for looking like that and making me cry with laughter.'

'Thank you very much, Soph; ... that's a bit much from the sugar- plum fairy.' ...

'Now you two,' Mother intervened; 'I hope you're ready. ... They don't like people being late. It's bad manners.'

Mother paused to attach a pearl ear-ring and continued. 'As it's a proper ball I want you to look after your sister, Tim; make sure she's not left out of the dancing; especially the reels.'

'Mother,' Sophie protested, 'I'm a big girl now.'

'You can say that again,' said Tim.

'You know where you can put yourself,' Sophie retorted; and I don't want you dancing with me, least of all looking like that! Everybody'll think I'm a complete wet. I'll be fine with Cam and Francesca!'

'I really don't have to dance with her anymore, Mother,' added Tim. 'Her spots have gone.'

'I could murder you,' snapped Sophie, glaring at him; 'you're really the ….'

'Enough!' cried Mother. 'You really are in a bad mood, Tim and you're being very unkind. … You will drive the Minx carefully, wont you?'

'Yes, Mother.'

'I really don't know how you'll get them all in.'

'Well they wouldn't fit in the Minor.'

'My God! I nearly forgot,' exclaimed Mother, opening a drawer of her dressing table. 'The laurel wreath; I've sprayed it in gold.' She placed it on Tim's head and stood back. 'There; the finishing touch; laurel for heroes and I hope you'll behave like one.'

Half an hour later Tim was in town, driving slowly uphill towards the square. Mother's green Hillman Minx was making heavy weather of its load. Rhyd sat sprawled in the passenger seat and, in the back, Sophie, Francesca and James, with

Camilla perched on his knees, were crammed together.

'You're probably finding my sister a bit of a weight, James,' said Rhyd casually.

'You know what you can do with yourself!' Camilla's riposte came quickly. Rhyd turned his attention to Tim, tweaking his toga. 'You look a real knob in that.'

'Bugger off, Rhyd,' muttered Tim, correcting the angle of the laurel wreath which had started to droop over one eye.

'Now,' said Rhyd, producing the bottle of Gordons he had stowed under his seat; 'the important business. ... There'll be loads of orange juice there so, every now and then, on a signal from me, fall in and bring your orange juices out to the car park and we can perk them up a bit; but remember to dump any hangers on beforehand' ...

They had just passed a junction of two streets when Camilla shouted 'Look out Tim; a policeman's waving you down.'

'Bugger,' exclaimed Tim under his breath, as he pondered the possibility of driving on. ...

'Tim, you've got to stop,' shouted Sophie. 'He'll have got the number.' Tim drew into a parking space and wound down his window.

The constable, who had caught up with them, looked down at Tim and immediately recoiled. 'Do you mind standing out, sir?' Tim got out of the car and stood in the street. Other vehicles were passing, hooting in derision.

'Well, I must say, sir,' continued the officer, 'when I first saw you I thought you were improperly dressed; exposing yourself in a public place.'

'I'm going to a fancy dress party,' explained Tim, sheepishly. 'I'm supposed to be a Roman Senator.'

'Really; and there was me thinking that you were dressed like that all the time, sir!' An explosion of half suppressed giggles came from the back of the Minx. The constable leaned down and peered in; then straightened up and looked Tim in the eye. 'And what, may I ask, are the young ladies supposed to be?'

'Vestal virgins.'

'I should certainly hope so,' said the officer, thoughtfully.

The Minx was rocking with the abandoned laughter of its occupants. The constable looked in again, sniffed loudly and glared at Rhyd. 'This is no laughing matter, sir. I saw you waving a bottle back there in a motor vehicle while it was in motion on the public highway.'

'Yes,' replied Rhyd, producing the Gordons; 'but we haven't been drinking it, officer. Look – It's unopened.'

'And how old are you, young man, to be in charge of a bottle of spirits?'

'Old enough to be in Oxford,' declared Rhyd, triumphally.

'I'll have you know,' said the constable, looking puzzled, 'that I would be taken to Cardiff when I was a young fellow like you.'

Tim, whose extremities were now turning blue and who had been at the receiving end of several whistles and 'V' signs, was relieved to see that they had been joined by a police sergeant. He looked Tim up and down, grinned at him and gestured him back into the car. 'If you stay on the street any longer, sir you'll catch your death of cold and you've already become a traffic hazard.' Tim gratefully got into the driver's seat. The sergeant peered down at him. 'You're a

Barrington-Lewis, aren't you?'

'Yes,' admitted Tim, under his breath, unhappy at being identified.

'My wife thinks the world of your mother and the way she runs the WI. ... Now,' continued the sergeant, stroking his chin, 'let me guess – you're on your way to the fancy dress at The Manor. ... I don't know; you young things always gallivanting about; ... and a bit of advice, sir; I should wear a cloak if I were you. The Romans would on an evening like this and we can't have you ending up in hospital, can we. ... Now off you go and enjoy yourselves – and drive carefully!'

Their destination, a survivor of the ravages of post war taxation and which had, so far, remained in aristocratic hands, was a large mansion dating from earlier times but substantially built upon and extended in the Regency and Victorian periods. Protected on three sides by sloping woodland, its front facade overlooked the sea to the North-West from which a cold wind blew. Tim dropped his passengers off at steps leading up to the main entrance and then parked the car as near as he could. Upon admission to the ballroom he knew that his worst fears had been realised. Most mothers had taken the easy and more expensive way out – hiring appropriate costumes for their offspring. Rhyd and James were in cloaks and tunics with plastic short swords and did not look out of place. Rhyd, with his saturnine looks and mischievous, mocking eyes, was already surrounded by a group of young girls. The others had disappeared, possibly disowning him. A barely recognizable "rock around the clock" was being played by an elderly band set on a podium between two pil-

lars at the far end. Young girls were twirling gracefully in
pleated dresses under the watchful eyes of their mothers;
boys stomping about and looking bashful; some parents joining in, bending and flailing; looking ridiculous. …

'Hail citizen!'

Tim swung round, coming face to face with a plump, soft-
featured man taller than himself. Wearing a magnificent robe
and dragging a long train he held, in his right hand, a golden
rod with an eagle on top. He reached out and adjusted Tim's
laurel wreath. 'There; that looks better. It was definitely at the
wrong angle and not befitting the dignity of Rome.'

'What are you supposed to be?' asked Tim, beginning to
feel put out.

'Your emperor, dear boy,' the man declaimed, his voice
rising to falsetto; 'and you may kiss my hand.' Tim noticed
the soft flesh of a finger bulging either side of a massive ring
extended towards him and was considering his options when
James tapped him on the shoulder and drew him away. …

'Who the hell was that?' shouted Tim, watching the "emperor" drift towards the dance floor.

'Keep your voice down,' whispered James; 'He's Sir Harry's
nephew; as camp as a boy scouts tent, apparently!'

'Bloody hell,' exclaimed Tim, looking about him. 'He's a
bit old for this lot.'

'Tim; we are old for this lot; or haven't you noticed. Come
on, let's get a drink.'

'What about Rhyd?'

'Don't worry about him. You've got the key.' …

Tim was feeling better after a large gin and orange. He offered a cigarette to James and they both lit up. He groped for the bottle. 'Shall we have another?'

'What with?' asked James, winding down the window to release the smoke. ... 'How's your course going?'

'OK, I suppose; it comes in the post.'

'Got some friends up there; any girls?'

Tim hesitated. 'I suppose I have a girlfriend ... if you could call it that.'

'What's she like?'

'Can you keep a secret?'

'Yes, of course; ... but why do you want to keep it quiet?'

Tim hesitated. 'She's older than me; she's married ... and I've been to bed with her.'

'What the hell,' gasped James. ... 'How did you meet her?'

In the gloom Tim was aware that James was observing him closely. 'She sort of arranged it. ... It's only happened once.'

'When?'

'About a month ago.'

'Have you heard from her since?'

'Nothing; ... she cried a lot and I never got to know why. ... She hardly said a word. ... Perhaps she thought I was no good.'

'I wouldn't think that, Tim. Women can be weird. The girls at Durham seem to be one big tease − all the way to the bed-room door and then they slam it in your face. ... Did you know that Rhyd's girlfriend's dropped him?'

'No; why?'

'He's not telling.'

'Poor Rhyd,' said Tim, ashamed at the worm of satisfaction stirring within him.

'So cheer up; you're obviously learning more about life than either Rhyd or me.'

'The trouble is, James, she's hooked me; ... left me aching to see her again. ... The last few weeks have been hell. Every time there's a message for me in the office my heart misses a beat. ... Do you think I should try to contact her? I could probably find a reason.'

'If she hasn't tried to contact you, I should leave it. ... What about the husband?'

'Doesn't know; ... at least I hope he doesn't know.'

'Leave it at that then; ... or you could get into deep water.'

'I need a drink.'

'I've got an idea,' said James, chucking his cigarette end out of the window. 'We put a big dose of gin in our glasses now and sneak some orange over it when we get inside.'

'Good thinking. ... Tell you what, James; before I go back to work I'll take you and Rhyd to a pub I've been to; right in the middle of nowhere; old fashioned like some crumby cottage with a weird landlady; but the beer is amazing!'

'You can count me in and I've never known Rhyd turn down an offer to visit licensed premises,' said James, turning on the courtesy light and looking Tim up and down; 'and you can't go back in there with your droopy sheet. You look like Ghandi; and those are your own sandals, aren't they?'

'All I've got is this,' said Tim, reaching for the rug which Mother had slipped into the back of the car. ...

Tim and James returned to the ballroom unnoticed, topped up their gins and stood with their backs to a log fire. Tim was feeling less exposed. James had attached the rug to his shoulders, allowing it to hang down his back; warming him in the manner of a cloak.

Before they could move the "emperor" was upon them. 'A garment of sorts, I suppose,' he cried, blinking at Tim; 'but, I perceive, you are posted to the furthest point of empire – Hadrian's wall.' With a mocking laugh he swept away from them.

'What was all that about?' shouted Tim above the din of the band doing what they could with a Buddy Holly number.

'He's right though, the clever bugger," James was laughing and pointing, 'your rug; it's a tartan.' ...

'They're barely out of nappies in here!' shouted Rhyd, coming towards them with the girls in tow; 'time for a drink.' He sniffed at Tim's glass. 'You've been at my gin you blighters; you cads!'

'We couldn't find you,' said Tim.

'You never bothered; you sneaky buggers! You ...'

'Come on Rhyd,' said Camilla, 'we're practically dying of thirst in here; and we're getting bored, aren't we Soph?'

'You bet. I'm totally fed up with being a vestal virgin,' declared Sophie, gesturing towards the dancing. 'They're all thirteen or fourteen or positively ancient! It's embarrassing,' ...

On the way out Tim stood between the pillars of the main entrance. He took a deep breath. He was glad he had broken his silence. James would, at least, keep his mouth shut. The burden of uncertainty and of longing had been a lonely business and now, at least, there was someone he could talk to; someone he could share it with; but not all of it. That would be impossible. ... James was right, of course, to suggest he leave things be but James had not been with her. The ache was still there; the thought that, like a siren, she was waiting for him; beckoning unseen. ... The wind was blowing hard, filling his lungs, bullying at the trees around him, carrying salt on its breath. He could hear the sea – brooding; dark under the night sky; whispering. ...

'What the hell are you waiting for, Tim?' Rhyd was calling from the car. ...

On the following Friday evening Tim, Rhyd and James sat in the Tafarn Bach. Tim had made good on his promise and had driven them there in the minor. The reluctant coming of spring had clothed the narrow cwm in shy greens, softening the stark outlines of the pub, concealing the bare bones of winter and the ugliness of fallen trees. They were sharing their first jug of beer and had concluded that Tim's recommendation had been sound. They sat in a group around the table nearest the fireplace, observed silently by three other patrons of the place.

'I wish she'd light it,' muttered Rhyd, looking at the empty grate. 'It's cold in here.' As if waiting for a cue Maggie came in, carrying a bucket, beamed at Rhyd and proceeded to lay and light the fire. 'Do you know what this is?' asked the lady, looking up at him and holding one of the coals.

'It's coal,' said Rhyd, looking puzzled.

'It's pele; coal dust and cement. I make it with my own hands; much cheaper than coal and you will see it burns well; gives off a lot of heat.'

'Good,' said Rhyd, in one of those rare moments when it

seemed he was out of his depth ...

By the time darkness had covered the valley and blacked out the window, Tim and James had made the acquaintance of the three others – a builder, a plasterer and a farmer. They had shared a jug together and were now in lively conversation. The farmer leaned forward. 'I think she fancies him,' he whispered, nodding in the direction of the fireplace where Rhyd sat trapped between Maggie and the chimney breast. Tim looked across at Rhyd. Their eyes met briefly, Rhyd's spelling out the desperation of one whose breeding would not allow the breaking off of a conversation with a lady, in particular his hostess, without the intervention of a third party. Tim suggested that he might join them but was promptly discouraged by his companions who had intimated that, in no time, he, himself might become the object of her affections. 'She's a widow, you see; been in the circus they say,' whispered the builder with a wicked grin, 'and it can be very lonely up here. ... I could see her eying him through the beer hatch as soon as the three of you came in. It must be love at first sight.' The whole company rocked with laughter as Rhyd, looking resentful, rose unsteadily from his table. Watched closely by Maggie he made for the front door.

'He's probably going to the toilet,' commented the plasterer; 'must be bursting after all that beer she's been giving him.' Tim and James glanced at one another, believing that this might also be a way for him to break free.

'I hope he can find his way,' said the builder. 'There's no light there, you see.'...

Rhyd was a long time returning but Maggie had been too

crafty for him, lying in wait at the door with a fresh jug poured in readiness. Now she was caressing his forehead. ...

'Looks like he's got a graze,' said Tim, feeling concerned.

'May'be he's walked into the lavatory door,' suggested James, with a wink.

'There is no door,' intoned the builder solemnly. 'I have offered to make her one at cost price and put a light in but she says no. ... She says everyone will be using it.'

'Well, I'm afraid I've got to use it now,' said Tim, standing up.

'I'll come with you,' said James, not wanting to risk the adventure alone.

'You go carefully boys,' called the farmer. 'It's as black as hell in there!'

As they passed Rhyd he did not seem to notice them; his back hunched and his eyes glazed having, presumably, taken refuge in sufficient alcohol to blot out all care as to who he was with or what he was doing. Maggie, rolling another cigarette, was still talking to him; touching his hand. ... The pathway to the 'toilet' was uneven. Tim had negotiated it on his previous visit but while there was still some daylight and when he was not inebriated. The facilities at night turned out to be dire – a concrete shed, its interior cloaked in stygian darkness and stinking of urine. It was taking time for Tim and James to find their bearings. ...

'Bloody hell,' cried James, 'I think I'm standing in a lake of piss. Which wall do I piss against, Tim?'

'I hope you are not going to piss on me,' came a deep voice from the gloom.

'Crikey Tim!' cried James. 'We've got company.'

'I'm sorry if we've disturbed you,' said Tim to the darkness. 'We can't see a thing.'

'Most who come here,' intoned the voice, 'light up a pipe or a fag. ... I'm out at the moment.'

'Have one of mine,' said Tim, finding his packet and offering it to the shadow in front of him. A hand groped for a cigarette and a match struck light into the gloom. The man's face in the glow was furrowed and weathered but his eyes had the twinkle of laughter in them. 'Gave you boys a fright, did I? Thought I was a ghost, then?'

'You weren't in the pub,' said Tim.

'I have just arrived for a late one. ... Nice to have met you,' said the man, disappearing into the night. ... On their way back to the pub Tim and James stopped on the pathway, swaying; laughing so loud that their voices filled the still valley. ...

The journey home was not uneventful. Tim was determined to drive with extreme caution upon the basis that he shouldn't be driving at all. His concentration was not helped by Rhyd who was slumped in the passenger seat. 'You swine; you bloody swine, both of you,' he slurred; 'leaving me high and dry with that hag!'

'We thought we should congratulate you upon your new girlfriend,' crowed James from the back. 'She's obviously very taken with you.'

'Bugger off, James; ... bugger off Tim. ... You saw me looking at you; trying to shake her off but you did nothing; bugger all; ... left me high and dry. ... Got no idea what she was rabbiting on about; never stopped. ... She was all over me; ...

old enough to be my mother! ... I'm going to be sick!' Tim slammed his foot on the brake, reached over and flung the door open – just in time. ...

Mother woke Tim to tell him off. Rhyd's parents had been far from pleased that he had been unceremoniously dumped in their porch and the bell rung. By the time his mother had come to the door the Minor had disappeared. Rhyd had been escorted upstairs by his mother and father but this had not been the end of their problems. He had passed out in the lavatory and become wedged between the pan and the wall. Both parents had had to tug at his legs in order to liberate him. ... Even though his head was sore Tim couldn't stop laughing.

'It's no laughing matter, Tim,' cried Mother; 'you and James leaving him like that. ... It's not like you. Perhaps it's just as well you're going back on Sunday; plenty of work to keep you out of mischief.'

# CHAPTER 10

Tim's encounters with the Reverend Ebenezer happened regularly on Thursday evenings between six and eight. Discovering that the old man, who dwelt in a house full of ticking clocks, was a stickler for time, Tim would drive there direct from work rather than be late. ... When the farm had dried out in the strengthening heat of the sun Gramp had suggested he try the footpath which crossed the farm; then passed through a wood and wound down the valley to join the narrow lane close to The Reverend's house. This was by way of a short cut which would be pleasant exercise in the Summer and enable Mam to give him tea and cake before he went. Early in May Geraint, who had some hay to collect, had taken him on his tractor to his tutor's house en-route, enabling him to explore his way home on foot. ...

His Welsh lesson over Tim had climbed the first section – a green lane with a steep gradient, twisting and turning between high stone and earth banks overhung by oak and beech trees – closing out the sky; casting a zebra light. Further up, tangled gorse in full, buttery bloom clung to broken banks – bright in the evening sun. Tim stopped at the top and looked down at the house he had come from – trim, stone built with brick quoins, regular windows, a slated roof and with a chimney at either end. To the rear was a tidy vegetable garden. If the old man was ever guilty of the sin of pride then this would be it – the neat, weed free rows of potatoes, beans and onions enclosed by a manicured hedge. Tim would be shown their progress at the end of each visit. ...

In the light of his slow progress he had been wondering whether to discontinue lessons but the old man had been very patient and encouraging. The cost was negligible and a subtle, unspoken attachment had emerged from their struggles with the language. He would sit at the old man's desk in a damp room full of musty books and attempt unseen translations and answers to questions in Welsh, many of them based upon Biblical texts. These, he suspected, were part of the old man's plan to save him for Jesus as Gramp had suggested. Samuel, the cat, would sit with Tim as he worked – a sign, according to his tutor, of his essential goodness. Samuel, apparently, would not hang about in the company of out and out sinners but Tim had wondered whether, in the circumstances, the cat's judgement was skewed. When he had done his best with the written work he would be taken to the kitchen for a cup of tea and two Welsh cakes. This routine, in spite of his protestations that he was going home to a hot supper at the hands of Mam, had become established and was, he suspected, not based upon his need but the old man's unswerving belief that no one who came into his house should ever leave it without refreshment. He had found a good excuse to cover his insistence; that these spells in the kitchen were an opportunity for some polite conversation in Welsh; experiences which, for Tim, had, more often than not, been excruciating. ...

He turned away and made for the trees. Gramp had told him of the bluebells – a phantom haze of kingfisher light, their scent beguiling, sweet and sensuous; drawing him in. He stopped in a clearing and looked up at an opalescent sky. He closed his eyes – breathing in the perfume of this insubstantial heaven upon earth which would soon be gone. ... On the far side of the wood the path followed a contour across the slope of Gramp's land. Above him cattle and sheep grazed in meadows turned gold in the evening sun and divided by hedges white with May. Below him whole fields were shut off for hay to be taken in June if the weather would allow. The farm's boundary lay at the bottom of the valley where a brook ran unseen within a slip of woodland and scrub which followed its course. On the far side, steep slopes, falling into shadow, rose to bright pastures and a spine of rocks where sheep grazed. ...

Early the following Monday morning Tim was standing in the market, waiting for the Brig who, it seemed, had been trapped into conversation by a group of grey men on the far side of the pig pens. Tim leaned on his thumbstick, adjusted his cap and looked about him; at the men bawling and waving sticks; the cars, new and old; some with trailers attached and the cattle lorries coming and going. ... A large Austin, a small hole wiped in the condensation of its windscreen, had, somehow, made it to the sheep pens. Now its owner, a stout man with a cap perched jauntily on the back of his head and shouting in a squeaky voice, was supervising the evacuation of half a dozen well grown lambs from its back seat. ... Over the weeks and months he had been getting used to his spells in this place – its sights, its sounds and its smells. He had even got used to the Brig's casual way of selling. He was still sketchy on the names of buyers but they had become aware of his deficiencies and were being co-operative. Today, in the bright sun of a May morning, he felt part of this essential meeting place; this cauldron of deals, of buying and selling; the financial heart and lifeblood of an entire farming community; a meeting place for those who laboured in remote valleys or on lonely hills. ... Some passers-by were waving at him and he was waving back, knowing them as purchasers of pigs or a friendly face in "The Contented Cow." ...

'Tim!' Boz was shouting from the door of the hut, his right hand raised, fingers and thumb down to the top of his head in the manner of an officer gathering his men. Tim went over to him at the double.

'You know I promised you a go at auctioneering,' said Boz, with a smile. ... 'Well this is it; more out of necessity than kindness, I'm afraid.'

'But the Brig's here,' said Tim, his pulse quickening.

'It's not the pigs, it's the calves. ... Ben's phoned in. He's wedded to the toilet, I gather. ... I'm with the heifers and calves at heel in the main ring; John's with the sheep and the Brig's with the pigs. ... There's no one for the calves. ... Can you do it?'

'I'll try,' murmured Tim, feeling panic setting in, 'but I don't know anybody there.'

'You'll have Teg to clerk for you,' countered Boz.

'What about the pigs?'

'The Brig can have Dai. Eleri can do the running. All sorted'

The calf ring, on first acquaintance, was an intimidating place; a circle formed in tubular railing under a high canopy of corrugated iron, rattling in the breeze. There were access and exit ways either side of the "box", an open-fronted wooden shed designed to accommodate the auctioneer and his clerk. The sight of Teg was comforting. The sight of the restless crowd pushing against the railings was not. The sale had been delayed. Some were eying him suspiciously; others were in groups, muttering. Tim turned to Teg who was organising his sale sheets. 'Is there a microphone?'

'No, Mr Tim; it's voice or nothing here.'

'I don't know the first thing about calves.'

'Don't worry, Mr Tim,' said Teg comfortingly, waving his papers, 'it's all here; I'll tell you as they come in. We had better start now. ... They don't like waiting.'

Tim took a deep breath and launched in. 'Well, ladies and gentlemen, we're ready to start the sale and ...'

'Are there any ladies here?' a wit piped up from the crowd.

'Yes there are,' came the voice of a woman at the back; 'and the young gentleman is well mannered enough to mention us; so leave him be!'

Tim smiled nervously at the lady and continued. 'I'm standing in today for Mr Jones who is unfortunately indisposed.'

'Stuck in the toilet,' came the wit's voice again.

'I'm sure we all wish him a speedy recovery,' Tim continued against ribald laughter; then called for the first lot. A thin, brown coated calf entered the ring with its owner – a wiry, shifty looking, cock-eyed man with a bent and dripping nose.

'What's that?' asked Tim in alarm, leaning over to Teg.

'A three month old roan cross-shorthorn dairy calf,' whispered Teg; 'from the wilderness and not in good condition. You won't get much for that, Mr Tim. Start it at five pounds.' ... Tim did and, after taking bids, brought his gavel down at seven.

'Well done, Mr Tim; no more than it was worth,' muttered Teg.

The sale proceeded in the same manner, Tim discovering that his fear of missing any of the nods, winks, stick tapping and cap shifting was unfounded. It appeared that a miraculous chemistry existed between auctioneer and bidder that left no doubt of intent; something in the meeting of eyes that not even a clerk would spot. ... They had made good progress when, according to Teg, a well grown cross-Hereford beef calf entered the ring. A huge man with a bulging red face, who had pushed his way to the front, clambered over the railings and stood in the ring.

'Should he be doing that?' whispered Tim.

'He's a butcher,' said Teg. 'We're on the beef calves now. ... He does this every week but he buys a lot. Leave him be but watch him. ... He gets up to tricks!'

The calf had gone to twenty five pounds when the big butcher looked at another bidder, winked, reached into the pocket of his dust jacket, took out a coin and tossed it. ...

'Stop the bidding, Mr Tim,' whispered Teg, tapping him on the arm. 'He's tossing in the ring. You'll have to stop him.' Tim was feeling desperate at the interruption of what seemed to be going so well and how the hell was he going to tell the giant who was already looking hostile. ...

'Teg, I can't tell him to stop tossing – not here. He might be offended.'

'You have to, Mr Tim,' Teg insisted, unaware of any other implications, 'because it's against the law. ... Tossing in the ring is in contravention of the Auction and Bidding Agreements Act 1927!' The stoppage was causing restlessness in the crowd. Tim decided to be diplomatic and call the man up to the "box" in Welsh. The use of his native tongue might serve to impress him; make him compliant. ...'Gwregysu dy lwynau ac dewch ataf Fi,' said Tim, breathlessly, hoping that he had found the words which would bring the butcher to him. The shouting and grumbling of the crowd was replaced by a respectful silence. The big man looked stunned; in some way bettered as if he had received a command from a higher authority. He came up to the "box" without argument, his small eyes porcine, quizzical. Tim took a deep breath. 'No tossing; ... you mustn't toss coins in the ring,' he blurted. The crowd greeted his admonition with abandoned laughter. The wit was at it again. 'He's training to be a Minister, for sure.'... There was more laughter which showed no signs of stopping. The giant winked at him, pushed his cap to the back of his bald head, put his coin in his pocket and returned to his place. Tim turned to Teg, who had remained silent during the commotion, and whispered 'did I say anything wrong?'

'As far as I could tell your Welsh was coming from different parts of  the Good Book, Mr Tim; probably from your lessons with The Reverend Ebenezer.'

'God! What did I say?'

'"Gird up thy loins and come unto me," it sounded like and your pronunciation is improving if I may say,' said Teg, smiling; 'and it wasn't what he was expecting. I don't think he'll be tossing any more today.' …

They were over half way when a large, Friesian heifer calf came into the ring, herded by a fresh faced girl in green over-alls who looked up at Tim and smiled. At the same time the "box" door opened and an elderly man entered, breathing noisily and smoking a roll up. …

'Is he supposed to be here?' whispered Tim, feeling un-easy with the presence beside him.

'He's her grandfather, Mr Tim … and the calf's a good one. He'll probably be offering "luck money."'

'What's that?'

'Something for the buyer; an inducement; pushes the bid-ding.'

Tim proceeded to sell the calf. When the bidding flagged the man waved a ten shilling note in the air – shouting some-thing in Welsh, his voice surprisingly strong. … Tim, having been stopped in his tracks, found that the bidding was com-ing again – raising the price. At the fall of his gavel the man muttered 'good boy,' grabbed his left hand from behind, pressed something into his palm and disappeared. When Tim opened his hand he found a crumpled ten shilling note. 'What do I do with this, Teg?'

'Keep it, Mr Tim. That's the other half; the auctioneer's "luck money." He thinks you did well for him; got a really good price.'

'This doesn't happen with the pigs.'

'The Brig won't have it, Mr Tim.' …

When the sale was over Tim was given a small round of applause.

'If I may be permitted to say,' said Teg, gathering up the remaining sale sheets, 'I think you should be well pleased with your performance.'

It had felt like a performance, the script made up as you went along but here there were real, not imagined consequences. 'Teg, what will become of the first lot; that thin little calf?'

'Pitiful creature, really; but she will be fine, Mr Tim; don't you worry. She's a dairy calf and gone to a good home. They'll bring her on; put some weight on her; then she'll become a follower in their dairy herd. She'll probably make a good cow in their hands.' ...

As they walked to the hut a dumpy man with a large calf on a tether shouted. 'You can come back anytime, English gent; never had so many laughs at a sale; and you got good prices!'

'I already have news from the front, Tim,' said Boz, following them into the hut and dumping a bundle of papers on the counter. 'You made a big impression out there.'

'I think I made quite a few mistakes; ... and I'm sure I've offended people with my efforts at Welsh; a bit Biblical apparently.'

'You don't want to worry about that. By now they'll have guessed you've been having lessons with old Ebenezer and that would explain everything. There's nothing they don't know round here.'

'I couldn't have done it without Teg,'

'Mr Tim,' intoned Teg, 'is a born auctioneer.'

Tim looked down, aware that the girls were watching him; not wanting to take too much praise; wanting to hide the pride which was burgeoning within him; mindful that, next time, he might not be so lucky. They had spoken of "beginners luck" with young auctioneers when the crowd and the dealers had been merciful but something had happened in that ring. He knew that he had got the crowd's attention. He was not what they were expecting. Mother had told him that his voice, when raised, was an inheritance from his father. Precise, clear, commanding and stentorian when needed, its resonance had made him unafraid. ...

Tim returned to the drawing office. Jim was at his desk, puffing at his pipe and studying a plan. 'This is the one you want,' he said, reaching into a wicker basket for a green cardboard file, fraying at the edges. 'I borrowed it from the Brig; like getting blood out of a stone. You'd better look at it now. He wants it back by five at the latest. ...Is there a problem up there?'

'No,' said Tim lightly; 'just wanted to be sure that my interpretation of the boundaries was correct. The Brig keeps on about trespass.'

'I'll get you a mug of tea while you look at it; had a busy day in the market by the look of you.'

Tim went to his desk and opened the file. It was not the plan he wanted to look at but the tenancy agreement to which it was attached. Discreet inquiry around the office had revealed nothing but a surname. Even Teg had failed to come up with the answer. If he asked the Brig there would be questions. The agreement was a last resort but would be useless if it wasn't in joint names. Holding his breath he read the first recital and there she was – "Julia."'...

# CHAPTER 11

Rain in June had delayed the taking of hay and made Geraint morose. Suppers with him had become melancholy affairs as the showers came and went. He would speak infrequently and then only to curse the weather or grumble about what might be lost. Geraint's moods, according to Gramp, had always been governed by the elements; a relationship which, he had suggested, was common among country dwellers and farming people who considered the sun, the wind and the rain to have capricious personalities; to be feckless partners in their enterprises. More than once Tim had seen Geraint shaking his fist and muttering in Welsh at dark, approaching clouds.

The coming of July brought bright sunshine. Neighbours, who would normally take it in turns to help and be helped in their gathering, were working from dawn until dusk on their own farms, knowing that the coming of more rain could ruin the crop. Geraint had, fortunately, invested in some machinery for the gathering of hay in that this was the staple which would take their livestock through the long, winter months. As soon as the ground was dry enough he cut the hay, field by field, with the mower attached to his grey, Ferguson tractor. The crop, lying flat, had then to be turned to prevent it from going mouldy. Geraint's pride and joy was his baler which would pick up the windrows of sun dried hay, noisily compact them into bales, tie them with twine and drop them off at intervals. At this time the whole farm was mobilised by him. Every action was subject to his will – Gramp, Mam and Beth being called into service for gathering, lifting and stacking of bales in the two open-sided barns. Tim, whose help had not been requested upon the grounds that he was a guest with studies to get on with, volunteered, nevertheless, for duty in the evenings. Mam would drive the Ferguson, Gramp would line up the bales with a hook, Geraint would hoist them on to the trailer with a pitch fork and Beth and Tim would stack them ready to take back to the buildings. Tim found the experience invigorating – the heady, sweet smell of new-mown hay, the evening sun on his back, a cool, scented breeze falling from the steep shadows of Twll Hill and drifting down the valley. Sitting on the trailer, under an amber sky, he would quench his thirst with the misty cider made from the orchard windfalls by Gramp in the previous autumn and reserved for harvest time. In the latter stages they were joined by some jovial neighbours who made short work of stacking in the barns and had been patient enough to respond to Tim's efforts at speaking Welsh; politely lapsing into English when his vocabulary ran out.

Late one Monday evening, in the middle of July, the work was complete. As the men sat on bales, watching the sky in the west turn from scarlet to burnt orange and then to green, Mam and Beth brought home-baked bread, cheese and pickled onions. Gramp's casks of home brewed beer and cider were tapped. His tankard full, Geraint looked happy at last, grinning through the fine hay dust which clotted his dark eyes and stuck to the perspiration of his brow. *That's it, Tim,'* he boomed; '*we're right for the winter now.*'

'*Yes we are,*' Tim replied, aware that this was the first time the big man had addressed him in Welsh. He drained the second pint of cider Mam had poured for him. Its strength was becoming apparent. He leaned back against the bales, light headed and closed his eyes. He was feeling part of this other family; part of its culture, part of its struggles, the farm and its fortunes. Full barns of good hay had ensured their survival for another year; a comfort which would take them through the bleakest of winters. Back in June Geraint had told him that a spoilt hay crop could mean the end for them. The purchase of hay from elsewhere for the number of dairy cows and beef cattle they over-wintered would be ruinous. ...

Back in the kitchen Mam was in a high state of excitement. 'You'll never guess, Tim, .... Geraint has bought a television,' she cried.

'Total waste of money if you should ask me,' intoned Gramp.

'I was not asking you. I was telling Tim.'

'Has he got it working?' asked Tim, anxious to avoid a confrontation.

'That is the very point, Tim,' exclaimed Gramp; 'so far it is a blizzard in a box.'

'Beth swears she saw a face,' replied Mam, looking hurt; 'Geraint says he will put the aerial on the chimney; then who'll be laughing?'

'I will.'.

'They have a good picture at Pen Twll.'

'Because they are on a hill,' replied Gramp, triumphally.

'Thank God we are in a valley. Who wants a load of jumped up English buggers telling us what to do with our time. It is bad enough on the wireless.'

'Now you're insulting Tim,' snapped Mam, wagging a finger at him.

'No, I am not. His father was from Wales and he is taking the trouble to learn the language,' muttered Gramp, reaching into the chimney cupboard for a box of matches.

'You're not going to light a fire in the middle of July, are you,' exclaimed Mam, shaking her head in disbelief.

'What does it look like?' said the old man provocatively, bending over the grate, arranging twigs and paper. 'Not so much to warm us, Tim as to have something cheerful to look at. … When the hay is in winter is on its way.'

'He always likes to look on the gloomy side,' cried Mam, who had started to noisily wash the pots; 'just like Geraint but he won't admit it.'

'Where's Geraint?' asked Tim, wanting to create a diversion.

'Gone with the boys,' said Gramp; 'to celebrate.'

'And they have taken Beth with them,' grumbled Mam. 'She's already had too much cider. She gets flighty; it's not fitting.'

'Leave her be,' countered Gramp. 'The boys will look after her and they will not be late. They have a long day tomorrow.'

'But we've got the hay in,' said Tim.

'Not our hay,' sighed Gramp, poking at the fire. 'They are going to rescue a couple of silly young English buggers on a small farm down the valley. … The man has hair as long as

the woman's and she is dressed in rags most of the time. ...
People say they are not married. ... They cut their hay by
hand a fortnight ago and want to make ricks out of it in the
old fashioned way – just the two of them, would you believe.
If it is not turned and baled before the rain comes back it will
be lost.'

'Have they asked for help?'

'No; too proud probably; but the boys will not stand back
and watch them ruined. They reckon they can do it if they
get a dry day. ... Mind you, not all the English are daft. There
is a good man farming on the far side of Twll Hill. They say
he cannot abide filling up forms; considers it a waste of his
time; so,' Gramp started to cackle and suck on his pipe, 'guess
what he did? ... He added one elephant to his stock return
every year and it took the Ministry of Agriculture seven years
to spot it – so he proved something, didn't he?' Gramp
reached up for the bottle of whisky and two glasses. He sank
back, groaning, onto the sgiw. 'Duw, Geraint works us so hard
on the hay and every year it gets worse for me; ... Mari! ...
Fetch us some water, will you?' ... Come on, Tim; no more
cider for you; just a little one to help you sleep. ...'

Tim opened his eyes, suddenly awake; grateful that Gramp
had not seemed to notice his dozing off; aware that time had
passed; his mind half-filled with Gramp's tales of the gathering by hand of crops in his youth; a time when ruin stood
waiting at everyone's gate; when, to be dispossessed, meant
homelessness in the rain, ice or snow; destitution; the work-
house even, at the hands of uncaring governments. ... Now,
at least, there was the regular cheque from the Milk Marketing

Board to keep the wolf from the door. ...

'It is always the same with me,' continued Gramp. 'When the hay is in; when the year has turned I get the urge to write.'

'Have you written something recently?' asked Tim, anxious to keep the conversation away from himself.

'No, but I will do. ... It will not be like the poems I wrote when I was young; the poems that won the prizes.'

'Why not?'

'Because the fire has gone out. I had fire in me then; and that fire got into the language. ... There were some who said I was a grown man with the vision of a child ... looking at things as if it was for the first time. ... Life was hard then, particularly the winters; the fields covered in snow, minding their own business; the trees in the cwm like bleached bones; but, in that frost and in that stillness, something spoke to me; burned into my soul; inspired me. ... Ebenezer writes clever poems from his head; mine came from my heart.' Gramp hesitated, drawing on his pipe. 'You have that look on you sometimes, Tim. ... Contemplation is a lonely business.'...

In the morning a dry wind blew, bending the trees and battering the campion and cow parsley in the hedges as Tim drove to work. His head still ached – an unwelcome consequence of his poetic encounter with Gramp. In an effort to avoid reading one of his own offerings he had persuaded the old man to recite one of his prize winning efforts – a lengthy affair, delivered dramatically; its language, which he could not follow, rising and falling like a turbulent sea. ...

Tim knew that something was wrong as soon as he walked

into reception. The girls were not at their desks but stood in a group. Rhian and Ffion were crying. Eleri looked up, her eyes watering, her cheeks stained. 'Dai has passed away,' she sobbed; 'his heart gave out they say – in his sleep.'

The funeral, a week later, was at Salem, a blockhouse of a chapel bordering the farm Dai had once owned. The firm had closed for the afternoon as a gesture of respect and to allow its staff to attend and for whom seats had been reserved. Teg, in his black pinstripe and bowler, took Tim in the Riley. The graveyard was black with those who had come to pay their last respects. Ushered into the chapel Tim found himself sitting next to the Brig. They sat close to the front within sight of the coffin which had been set up under the pulpit. ... As Ministers came and went to extol the virtues of Dai, whose virtues Tim considered worth extolling, the Brig became more and more agitated. He leaned over and muttered. 'How many more. ... Can you understand any of them?'

'Only a bit, sir.'

The singing was a massive, uplifting sound upon which Tim imagined that Dai might be borne back to the Elysian fields of his beloved farm. Last verses were sung twice. In the final hymn the congregation were going for a third repetition.

'I cannot abide this obnoxious habit of prolonging the hymns,' growled the Brig; 'they're long enough already.'

'I think it's their way of ... not wanting to say goodbye, sir.'

'Goodbye to what, boy?'

'The hymn, I think and, of course, Dai, sir,' whispered Tim, feeling pleased that, as a result of his many conversations

157

with Gramp, he had acquired a knowledge of country ways which the Brig was in no position to dispute.

'He must be bored to death, poor fellow,' snorted the Brig, 'hearing all this, wherever he is.'…

Dai, in recognition of his failing health, had left a Will naming Tim as one of his bearers. As he and five other men bore the coffin past rows of sad faces towards the waiting hole of the grave, Tim's composure left him. He thought of the many unspoken kindnesses he had been shown by the man he carried; whose background and culture had been so different from his own; the man who had saved him from humiliation; who had encouraged him; helped set him on his way; who had never, in his hearing, blamed anyone for his own misfortunes in life; who had borne his afflictions with courage and good humour; who, instead, had counted his blessings. … As the tears rolled down his cheeks Tim felt hands reaching out from the crowd through which they slowly moved, touching him on his shoulder.

The journey back to the farm took them past the Reverend Ebenezer's house. Tim asked to be dropped where the footpath joined the lane. Teg protested that a black suit and shoes were not suitable apparel for a country walk but Tim insisted. … The wind had eased. He walked up the green lane, his black leather shoes twisting and turning uncomfortably on its uneven surface. He passed through the wood, its bluebells long gone – replaced by patches of bramble and wild garlic releasing its pungency as he trod upon it. He reached Gramp's land on the far side of the wood and stopped to look over the valley, its surface brindled by the transit of gathering clouds. He thought of Dai, who had been content to be called "The Runner" by the Brig; who had regarded his nick-name as a compliment; whose tortured body now lay cradled in the soil which had once been his labour and his love. ... Tim began to wonder whether, in this friendly landscape, the living and the dead could co-exist by footpath and style, among the crops, the cattle and the changing of the seasons. ... He walked on. The sun had found a hole in the thickening cloud – picking out the white farmhouse in a pristine light against the darkness of its surrounding fields.

# CHAPTER 12

B ack in April the firm had received instructions for what was going to be the stock-sale of the year. The tenant of the largest farm on the Twll Estate had decided to retire. By all accounts he had managed it profitably and well for the better part of his lifetime. Although under the management of the Brig, as agent for the Estate, it was known that these valuable instructions had been secured by means of the gentle urging and diplomacy of Teg who attended the same Chapel as the tenant and his family.

Early in August, six weeks before the sale was to take place, Boz and Tim stood at the door of a substantial, grey stone house which Tim thought to be more like a vicarage than a farmhouse. Enclosed by a kept garden it lay separate from its yard and buildings. … Their knock was answered by the tenant – a tall, wiry looking man with thinning, grey hair and kindly eyes; whose demeanour seemed more that of a retired academic than a farmer. They were welcomed indoors. There they sat at a table of scrubbed pinewood while tea and cakes were brought by the tenant's wife. Tim looked up to thank her. Her smile was gentle, caring; her appearance and manner a combination of elegance and homeliness. Tim sensed in her an intangible weariness; a relief; a letting go of burdens. … Conversation began in Welsh, the tenant's delivery silken and flowing; the language of one who has carried its meaning and its subtleties from the cradle. When he learned of Tim's lack he spoke in English with the precision and clarity of a gentleman.

Out on the yard plans were laid while Tim made notes. He looked about him. Buildings seemed better maintained and used than those on other estate farms he had visited. Behind the traditional ranges of stone and slate stood two modern covered yards, ready for over wintering of the cattle now out on their summer pastures. ... A red Morris Minor drove into the yard and pulled up beside a shed. A lanky girl, in dungarees and wellington boots and wearing a man's cap, got out and walked confidently towards them.

'This is my daughter, Fflur,' said the tenant, smiling broadly; 'she can't help being late.'

'Why are you speaking in English, dad?' she asked, her arms spread in inquisition.

'Because,' replied the tenant, nodding in Tim's direction, 'this young gentleman can't speak Welsh yet. He's still learning.'

Fflur wagged her head; then extended her hand. Tim felt it to be soft and warm; not the calloused hands of a farmer's daughter. He said nothing; smiled at her briefly; then looked down at his notes. When he looked up she had turned away. ...

Plans were made for the positioning of the sale ring, the washing, stalling and numbering of the cattle by the tenant's two farmhands and the lotting up. Miss Morgan and her accounts were to be installed in the farm office. With a sale of this magnitude she would need two assistants; one to find and present the invoices to buyers as they came to pay and another to make out their cheques when requested. Left to their own ponderous, copper plate writing, some of the older buyers would cause queues to form. The pride of the tenant's farming life was his pedigree herd of Freisian milking cows and their followers, carefully bred over the decades of his tenancy. Tim could see that the prospect of their break-up and dispersal was painful for him. There was a lingering sadness about him – the look of a man reluctant to quit his responsibilities – cows he had known since they were calves; cows he knew by name; cows who knew each others' ways; cows who had never left the farm. … Boz was being comforting and constructive. The Freisian Society had been informed. The cattle would be widely advertised, not only in the Twll Trumpet and the Rhywle Gazette but also in regional papers and the national farming press. The alternative of selling them in one lot as an established herd would yield a substantially lower price per cow. Big sums were paid by dairy farmers for two or three pedigree beasts to improve the milk yield and, ultimately, the conformity of their own herds.

They moved to the hay sheds where it was agreed that the tonnage of this year's crop, safely gathered in neatly stacked bales, be taken at valuation by an incoming tenant at Michaelmas. They walked the land under a veiled sun, observing the cattle. They filed past fields of barley – drifting in the warm, light breeze and to be taken at valuation as a harvested crop. They looked at the sheep grazing the tight, closely cropped pastures of the upper ground. Finally they inspected the farm machinery. Fordson and Ferguson tractors, a nearly new combine harvester, trailers, turners, balers, a seed drill and a plethora of other, smaller equipment had been gathered under cover – ready to be arranged in orderly lines on an adjacent field by the tenant and his men in advance of auction day. ...

'By the time we get through the livestock I'll be needing a rest,' said Boz. 'Jim can do the standing crops and the big stuff here. ... That leaves you, Tim, to see to the rest.'

Tim looked up from his notes. 'You mean auction it?'

'Yes,' said Boz, grinning at him; 'and some of the household furniture as well.'

Tim, sensing a moment of importance, glanced at Fflur. Their eyes met briefly, her delicate features questioning; an eyebrow raised; her lips pursed in a half smile. Tim looked away.

'Now,' said Boz; 'who's keeping the second book?'

'I am,' said Fflur, removing her cap and pushing back strands of hair which had been obscuring her face; 'and I'll be keeping an eye on the prices. They'd better be good.'

Tim, wondering whether her remark had been aimed at him, glanced at her again. She was laughing and looking away. ...


'Now that's going to be a sale to remember, Tim,' said Boz, cheerfully as the Landrover sped past high hedges bright with yellow rattle and honeysuckle. 'Good people they are; they'll have everything sorted for us; no problem.' ... Boz paused. 'What do you think of the daughter?'

'She's good looking.'

'Even in her farming clothes she looks a smasher.'

'I think she doesn't like me.'

'Ah, but she was looking at you, Tim,' countered Boz; 'she was watching you all the time.'

'I didn't notice,' said Tim, wondering why he hadn't.

'She wouldn't want you to notice. … She's a proud piece but I think she fancies you, Tim. I should get in there if I were you; and she's not stupid; … got a place in Aberystwyth.'…

Tim was grasping for a significance. He had been to Aberystwyth only once when Mother had first travelled to West Wales in search of cheaper property. As a bored twelve year old on a grey, January day he had been allowed to wander its pier while Mother attended to her business. Blanketed in a cold sea fog and uninhabited, the place had seemed drab; desolate even. Mother had given him some pocket money to spend on machines. After swallowing a quantity of pennies the claw in the glass case had selected a small doll which he had thrown into the sea in disgust. By the time Mother had caught up with him he was peering into a "what the butler saw" machine, pulling angrily at its handle. The bloody thing had jammed just as matters had got interesting. Mother had pulled him away and checked upon the object of his frustration. He had been frog-marched, blushing, to the car where, on the way home, Mother had told him that it wasn't nice to think of ladies with no clothes on. …

'Mind you, Tim,' said Boz, 'she is a bit of a "Nat."'

'What's that?'

'A Nationalist – mixing with some hot headed types, they say; getting worked up about road signs and forms not being in Welsh.' Boz paused and continued. 'They do have a point.'...

Back at the farmhouse a letter from Mother lay on the kitchen table. Tim took it up to his room and opened it. ...

*7th August 1959*

*Dearest Tim*

*I have heard from Friedrich at last. He says he is coming to stay the week after next to coincide with your holiday so that he can get to know you. I felt sure that you wouldn't mind. As Rhydian and James will be down I am inviting them and their families to dinner so that Friedrich can meet them properly; ... also the Merit-Owens. I definitely owe them hospitality. ... I was thinking of cold salmon. I know that you know people who could get one really fresh at a bargain price. We will need a big fish. Can I leave the negotiations to you? Sophie and I are very much looking forward to seeing you on the 17th. Friedrich arrives by train the day after.*

*With Much Love*

*Mother*

Tim put the letter down and groaned. For half of his holiday he would be stuck with looking after a total stranger; someone whose tenuous connection with the family was no more than a painful memory. Rhyd, James, their parents, everybody would be wondering where Friedrich fitted in. It could be really awkward. … He had been racking his brains for an excuse to see Fflur again and here was yet another complication. … His luck with women seemed to be doomed. She had given him no encouragement. She had seemed aloof, confident, haughty; almost dismissive but Boz's words had stuck in his mind. Was she testing him? If he didn't try to contact her would she think he was a drip? … Had that been the problem with Julia? Was she still waiting on that hillside; waiting for him to sum up the courage or had she simply tried him out and found him wanting? … He opened the drawer of his bedside cabinet and reached for the half bottle of whisky. There was barely a mouthful left. …

The next day he went to Miss Morgan's office. Billy, with a grin and a studied wink, willingly accepted his commission to get a salmon big enough to feed at least fourteen. The means of its entrapment were not discussed.

# CHAPTER 13

Friedrich was not what Tim was expecting although, in truth, he had not given much thought to the matter. The only photograph of his unwanted guest, enclosed with his letter to Mother, was a head-shot. In the flesh he towered above the few passengers alighting at Dewi Halt. His greeting was not the formal handshake anticipated but a bear-hug which almost lifted Tim off his feet. Blushing with embarrassment he found himself looking up at startlingly blue eyes peeping at him through long, blonde hair. As they walked to the Minor he noticed that Friedrich had a loping gait and a slight stoop which looked as if it had been acquired by continuously looking down at people.

Early the following morning Tim drove back to Rhywle to collect the salmon. Billy had coaxed it from the Rhyw the evening before; his task made easier by low water which had allowed him to spot and select a fish of just the right size from his favourite pool. Having timed the whole business to perfection Billy was in a high state of excitement, describing in rambling, unpunctuated sentences the unwanted details of his poaching prowess. His adventures had, apparently, ended in his favourite pub where everyone knew him and no one asked any questions. Returning home Tim parked in the driveway next to Mother's Minx. Feeling pleased with himself he removed the fish, wrapped in newspaper, from the boot of the Minor and carried it into the kitchen. Mother and Sophie were at the sink. 'Tant-tara,' cried Tim, holding out his parcel in triumph.

'Tim,' whispered Mother, wheeling round – her finger to her lips, 'he's a communist!'

'Who?'

'Friedrich.'

'He said something about it on the way back from the station.'

'You might have warned me.'

'I didn't think it was important.'

'It certainly is. He told me over his cornflakes. It was a terrible shock.'

'Reds not just under our beds but in them!' cried Sophie, stifling laughter.

'Sshh,' whispered Mother; 'it's not funny. Just think who's coming tonight. If he starts talking about Trotsky and Lenin we're done for. It'll be a disaster!' Mother paused to draw breath, her chest heaving in her distress. ...'If I had known of his political inclinations I would not have asked him to visit us,' she moaned. ...'Having an out and out communist in the house is absolutely awful; ... and I must say I am disappointed. His hair is a disgrace. It's like having a conversation with a blonde hedgehog; and I'm surprised his English isn't better. His letters seemed so fluent and ...'

'He probably got help with them,' said Tim, cutting in sharply, feeling peeved that his triumphal entrance had been spoiled by Friedrich's politics. 'He's doing science not languages and, whatever he's got, it's better than our German.' Tim dumped his parcel on the table and unwrapped it. ...

'What do you think of this?'

'"The News of the World,"' exclaimed Mother. 'Tim dear, you don't actually read it, do you?'

'No Mother,' sighed Tim in exasperation. 'Billy probably tries to.'

'Who's Billy?'

'He caught the fish.'

'It's so big; and silvery,' purred Mother, stroking its scales; 'just what we want … and, although I don't approve of his reading material, you tell this Billy from me that he's a very good fisherman. It took your dear father such a long time to persuade his first salmon to take the fly. …'

'Billy does know where to find them.'

'How much do I owe him?' asked Mother, reaching for her purse. 'I want to give you the money now before I forget.'

'He won't take any money, Mother.'

'Why not?'

'I offered and he refused. He says I'm his friend.'

'Well,' said Mother, with a deep sigh, putting her purse away; 'it looks as though he certainly is. … I will write him a letter of grateful thanks which you can give to him when you return to work.'

'I wouldn't bother.'

'It would be very impolite not to.'

'He probably won't read it, Mother.'

'I don't understand.'

'He has difficulty with words; that's all. …'

'I think we should cut the head off,' said Sophie, her face screwed up in disgust.

Mother was looking puzzled. 'What head, dear?'

'The fish; I can't bear the staring eye and that savage jaw! It looks as if it might bite.'

'What! Cut the head off a twenty pound cock salmon?' cried Tim.

'Why not?'

'Because it's simply not done Soph; ... not with a whole fish like this. You can cover it up with mayonnaise if you like.'

Over lunch Mother had expressed concern as to whether their guest would be properly dressed for dinner. In the afternoon Tim was detailed off with Friedrich to go through the contents of the one, amorphous canvas bag he had arrived with. The search revealed that the nearest thing to a suit was a crumpled velvet jacket in dark blue and a pair of black velvet trousers. They reported back to Mother in the kitchen.

'Friedrich,' she exclaimed, her eyes bulging in disbelief; 'where, in the name of Heaven, did you get those?'

'I vos getting zem in Berlin.'

'Well,' sighed Mother, shrugging her shoulders, 'you had better give them to me. I'll do my best to remove the creases and Tim can lend you a tie.'

'Dank you, Frau Lewis.'

'It is Mrs over here,' replied Mother tartly, 'and I am Mrs Barrington-Lewis. Do you understand?'

'I am already commanded completely, Mrs ... Barrington-Lewis,' replied Friedrich in the manner of an automaton and without apparent embarrassment.

'Mother,' whispered Tim, wanting to rescue Friedrich from the full glare of her displeasure; 'there's something you should know.'

'What?'

'Friedrich's brought six large bottles of Hock and a bottle of Schnapps. They were at the bottom of his bag. No wonder it weighed a ton. God knows how he got through customs!'

'You dear boy,' cried Mother, her mood softening; 'the hock will go so well with the salmon.' She checked suddenly and beamed at Friedrich. 'Is it for us?'

'For you my dear ozzer family; also ze schnapps,' declaimed Friedrich, putting his arm around Tim and squeezing his shoulder tight, 'vich I hope to share viz you und especially my new bruder Tim.'

'Now that is very thoughtful of you, Friedrich. ... We'll just have to do our best to make you as tidy as possible.'

'I vud like very much to be tidy for you, Mrs ... Barrington-Lewis.'

'Good; now what about your shoes?'

'The news there,' muttered Tim, 'is that he has the hiking boots he arrived in and what he's wearing now.'

'Sandals!' cried Mother in dismay. 'Tim you'll have to lend him a pair of your black shoes.'

'Have you seen the size of his feet, Mother?'

In the event Tim was put in charge of Friedrich's wardrobe with instructions to turn him out as best he could in the circumstances. In the final stages of his preparation Sophie was called in to advise on what to do with his hair. She combed it back into a small pigtail which she secured with a black velvet ribbon. This, at least, settled the problem of the unruly thatch obscuring his eyes, making him look gormless and having constantly to be gestured away but now Tim reckoned he looked like a survivor from Nelson's navy. There was also something feminine about the arrangement although the protruding line of Friedrich's jaw and his stubble spoke otherwise. …

Beyond midnight Tim was sitting at the kitchen table, his head cradled in his hands. Mother and Sophie were washing up. Friedrich, swaying to and fro and humming a tune that no one seemed to know, was wiping the plates dry; then stacking them noisily on the sideboard. 'Be careful with those, Friedrich,' cried Mother and, under her breath, 'I think you should do the glasses, Sophie; he's not very steady; and, as for Tim, he's obviously had far too much to drink. He'll have such a headache in the morning.'

'I already have,' mumbled Tim.

'You jolly well deserve it. …You kept on and on filling your own glass; and everyone else's. All the bottles are empty!'

'Well, they certainly enjoyed themselves,' chuckled Sophie. 'Cam said it was one of the best dinner parties she's been to with her parents; she'd never seen them so … relaxed. She and I had to help her mother get into their car!'

'It isn't done to intoxicate your guests,' Mother sighed; 'but, perhaps, on this occasion, it was a bit of a blessing.'…

This was the only reference that Mother had made so far concerning Tim's blunder. It had come with the first course. Felicity Merit-Owens, obviously carried away by the fact that Friedrich had kissed her hand upon their introduction, had asked him what his connection with the family was. He had, with a brutal honesty borne of a lack of vocabulary, told the truth. In the chaos of preparing Friedrich for the party Tim had forgotten to pass on the vital instruction from Mother that they were to say they were pen friends and no more. 'I'm sorry, Mother,' groaned Tim; 'I really am. It shouldn't have come out like that.'

Mother left the sink and stood beside him, her hand upon his shoulder. 'Well ... it's out now, my dearest boy,' she whispered, caressing his hair; 'and, in some way, I feel relieved of a burden.'...

Friedrich's revelation had caused Mother and Sophie to head for the kitchen on the pretext of getting the salmon ready. This had left Tim as the centre of attention in the dining room. Even Rhyd had been observing him sympathetically. Flushed with anger he had drained his glass and refilled it. The rest of the evening had been a blur. ... 'It's almost as if we're ashamed of what father did.'

'It was just such a very odd way to die in a war,' said Mother thoughtfully, rubbing her eyes. ... 'Did you hear what Rhydians's father said of it?'

'He said a lot.'

'I'll tell you when you're sober.'

Friedrich, apparently unaware of the family drama being played out in front of him and still humming, was about to start on the glasses. He tripped and steadied himself on the end of the table. 'Friedrich dear,' cried Mother in the stentorian voice she had always reserved for anyone south of Calais, 'I want you to leave the glasses for Sophie. ...There is something else you can do for me.'

'Vos is dat, Mrs Barrington-Lewis?'

'Roxy has been off her food today. She does this sometimes; rare for a spaniel. Could you please stand by her bowl and keep repeating "Pussy will have it." That usually works; particularly if the cat actually makes an appearance. Keep calling until Roxy starts eating.'

Friedrich, looking puzzled, took up his position and began chanting "Pussy vill ave it" in a manner more threatening than persuasive. By the time he had got into double figures his chanting had reached a crescendo.

'For God's sake,' shouted Tim, shaking himself from the doze which was overtaking him, 'put a sock in it, Friedrich! Can't you see she's scared of you? Look – she's cowering in her basket. She probably reckons you're the Gestapo!'

'That was uncalled for,' snapped Mother, rounding on Tim; ... 'anyway, where is Sylvester?'

'I don't know,' muttered Tim. 'Friedrich's probably scared him off too.'

'Enough of that; you can look for him; time you did something.'

'He's probably gone for a mouse.'

'Unlikely,' countered Mother, 'with all these leftovers about and we don't have any mice that I know of.'

Tim stood up and made his way unsteadily into the scullery. A minute later he was back in the kitchen. 'I've found him,' he said, propping himself against the door frame; 'no wonder he didn't come.'

'Why is that?' asked Mother, drying her hands.

'He's dead; ... in his bed; ... stone cold.'

Mother put her hand to her mouth. Sophie started to howl. ...

Ten minutes later Sophie was still sniffling into her handkerchief. ... 'We have a problem, Tim,' said Mother, looking agitated.

'Don't worry; I'll dig a hole for him tomorrow.'

'How could you?' cried Sophie.

'We can't leave him in his basket going off, Soph. You can choose where we put him.'

'Tim! you're being remarkably insensitive,' shouted Mother. 'Now listen or are you too drunk to care? ... Your salmon may have been poisoned!'

'Nonsense.'

'When Sophie and I came to get the salmon we found Sylvester helping himself. I practically wept.'

'How much had he eaten?'

'Several bites out of the upper side. ... You know how greedy he is ... or rather was.'

'We all ate the fish. No one found out.'

'Because Sophie and I made urgent repairs with mayonnaise while you were drinking yourself silly and Friedrich was telling everyone about Karl Marx. ... I must say that, tonight, all my worst nightmares seem to have coalesced into a single, dreadful reality.'

'There's nothing wrong with the fish, Mother.'

'How do you know?'

'I just do. It was fresh this morning.'

'This "Billy" person may have used some chemicals to catch it for all we know.'

'Billy's too twp for that.'

'I do wish you wouldn't use that word.'

'It's just a kinder way of saying he's a bit thick.'

'You're slurring your words. ... There's only one thing for

it,' said Mother, thoughtfully, 'we'll have to phone them all and tell them to make themselves sick.'

'You can't be serious.'.

'Yes I can. ... My conscience simply won't allow it; and we should make ourselves sick too,' declared Mother, turning to Friedrich. ... 'What do you think, Friedrich?'

'I sink you are correct, Mrs Barrington-Lewis. I vill be sick as soon as possible.'

'Are you sure he's got the point?' muttered Tim.

'He's been listening carefully, haven't you Friedrich?'

'I ave, Mrs Barrington-Lewis.'

'So, ghastly as the prospect is, we must tell them and soon. ... Oh God,' cried Mother, looking up at the clock. 'It's one o'clock in the morning. We must ...'

'Mother,' Sophie interrupted, 'shall we all just go to bed? Leave it till the morning. We'll be a laughing stock if we do this now and nothing happens.'

'Better to be a laughing stock than have the neighbourhood strewn with corpses. ... I'm sure they'll appreciate the warning.'

'They won't,' Tim groaned. 'It'll be so bloody embarrassing.'

'I'll pretend I didn't hear that,' said Mother, glaring at him; 'and do I take it you're not going to help your poor Mother out of a dreadful situation?'

'By doing what?'

'Phoning our guests and warning them,' said Mother, her eyes beginning to water. 'I feel too emotional to cope with that myself at the moment. It's just a simple message; that's all.'

'Mother,' replied Tim, raising his voice in exasperation, 'I'm not going to do it because it's ridiculous and tomorrow, when everyone's' OK, I'll look a complete idiot.'

'Well, I'm past caring,' cried Mother, waving her hands in the air, 'I really am; abandoned by my family.'

'I vill do zis for you, Mrs Barrington-Lewis,' declared Friedrich, stepping forward. 'I vill phone ze people.'

'Mother,' pleaded Tim, 'you can't let this happen.'

'Oh yes I can ... if my own son won't come to my aid.' Mother went to the sideboard, grabbed a pencil and a piece of paper; then wrote down a telephone number. 'Here we are, Friedrich dear. We'll start with the Rhys-Williams's. ... The telephone's in the hall. We'll leave the door open in case you need any assistance. Please tell them that I am too distressed by Sylvester's death to speak to them myself. ... Do you understand?'

'I understand completely, Mrs Barrington-Lewis.'


It seemed an age before the call was answered ... 'Allo; Friedrich he speak. It vos great pleasure to meet viz you.' ....

'Ze reason I phone now is to say zat Sylvester is stum.'...

'Sylvester is cat; he dead. Mrs Barrington-Lewis; she very sad.'...

'She say Sylvester eat salmon.' ...

'He take many bites out of fish. ... Then he die.' ...

177

'She say – you be sick immediately or you die also.' …

Mother was looking desperate. An obvious solution was beginning to take shape in the boozy ferment of Tim's mind. 'Lie Mother,' he whispered; 'for God's sake lie.'

'What do you mean?'

'Tell them that you gave Sylvester the leftovers.'

'Ah … the leftovers. … Why didn't I think of that,' cried Mother, racing to the phone. …

Tim woke in a sweat. Bright sunlight was lighting up his bed. He threw back the blankets and sat up. A dull, throbbing ache inhabited his forehead and the decaying fumes of the hock were still hanging about in the bridge of his nose. He sniffed, rubbed his eyes and looked about him. The alarm clock lay on the floor. Shoved off its table when it had attempted to rouse him at the usual hour of eight, its insistent clattering had continued to unwind slowly and dreadfully, leaving him in a fitful doze. Now its hands were pointing at ten thirty. A stiff breeze was chivvying at the window. He got up and lifted the bottom sash; then sat back on the bed, inhaling the salt freshness of the inshore wind. Beyond the familiar orchard and the sloping field the sea was in a wild mood, roughened by white horses; fast moving clouds patterning its surface, turning azure to aquamarine, indigo to pewter and gunmetal grey. Tim had grown to love this view; always changing with the weather; hinting at danger; a prospect which could never be taken for granted. His skippering of the small sailing dinghy, parked on the beach below, had taught him that the sea was a siren; that it kept its own counsel; that its alien gods were capricious, brooding and swelling; prone to sudden rages and, above all, neutral. They didn't care who took them on; whether you lived or died but that was the fun, the challenge, the adventure. …

Tim arrived in the kitchen at eleven o'clock.

'A very good morning to you, Tim,' declaimed Friedrich, standing to greet him.

'I've known better,' muttered Tim, envious of Friedrich's apparent capacity to avoid hangover. 'Any breakfast?'

'Breakfast has well and truly come and gone,' crowed Sophie, leaning against the Aga rail; 'but there's coffee. Friedrich's made some – German style. He had some in his bag; really strong.'

'How much more do you think we're going to find in that bag?' groaned Tim as he sank into a chair at the end of the table, supporting his head in his hands.

'This is what you need by the look of you,' said Sophie cheerfully, sliding a saucer-less cup in front of him. He sniffed at the powerful combination of ground bean and steam and took a sip. 'Where's Mother?'

'Outside – with the vet; and poor Sylvester.'

'Is she annoyed with me?'

'She thinks you were horribly drunk … and uncaring; and so do I. … I think she's got a bit of a headache as well as you but she's not making a fuss about it.'

'It is just like Nurnberg,' declared Friedrich; 've students ave parties all ze time. … Much bier, zen ze bad head und …'

'I'm sure you all have a wonderful time over there,' cried Sophie, 'putting poor little cats into boxes and waiting for them to die or not.'

'Ah Sophie; I vos talking of "Schroedinger's Cat". Ze cat, ze box, everysing is seoretical. It is ze great experiment of uncertainty. In your mind you put ze cat in ze box viz a radioactive isotope und ...'

'You don't have to go into all that again.'

'But, Sophie, it is not real,' continued Friedrich, warming to his subject. 'Now if ze isotope decays sufficient before you open ze box zen ze cyanide is released und ze cat dies. If decay does not happen enough before ze box is opened, zen ze cat lives ... but all zis is in ze mind only.'

'It's still a horrid idea; ... and how come that poor Sylvester dies just after you told everyone about this Schroedinger person? It's all very odd.'

'Give it a rest, Soph,' sighed Tim. ... 'How, in God's name, did all that come up last night?'

'Camilla; she vos asking many questions.'

'Well she would,' muttered Sophie; 'she'll be reading physics at Cambridge and she wants to be ahead of the rest already.'

'Miaow.'

'In the circumstances, Tim, that really is unkind.'

Tim looked up at his sister and grinned. For a moment her voice and her manner had become a reflection of Mother. Now her eyes were reddening; glaring at him; about to fill with tears. He was anxious to change the subject. 'Were you sick?'

'What do you mean?'

'Did you make yourself sick last night?'

'No, of course not. What a revolting thought?'

'It was Mother's suggestion.'

'Did you?'

'What do you think?'

'I vos sick,' announced Friedrich, solemnly. 'Your Mutter instructs me und so, before I go to ze bed, I go in der toilette und ...'

'We don't need to know what you did there, thank you Friedrich,' interrupted Sophie, her eyes closing in disgust.

'Ah Sophie but, because I vos sick, I have good ead today ... und, tonight, we go to meet viz your friends at ze Schitting Duck.'

'"Sitting Duck", said Tim, raising his voice above Sophie's mirth.

'I have said somesing funny, Tim?'

'Why the hell are we going there, Soph?' asked Tim, ignoring the question.

'Because you arranged it.'

'When?'

'Last night; at the party.'

'I don't remember firming up on it.'

'You did – when you were drunk. You said nine o'clock. They'll all be there and you want to go, don't you Friedrich?'

'Ya, Sophie. I very much like to meet viz your friends again.'

Mother came in from the scullery. Friedrich scrambled clumsily to his feet. Mother looked down at Tim. 'I must say that, in spite of his politics, our guest has beautiful manners.'

'This is home, Mother; and there are lots of spare chairs.'

'That's not the point,' said Mother, beaming at Friedrich and sitting in his chair; 'one should set an example or we'll all end up living in a jungle.'

'What does the vet say?' enquired Sophie.

'Oh; good news.'

'How can it possibly be good?'

'I know how close you were to dear Sylvester, darling but it appears that he died of a combination of old age and over eating.'

'No poison then, said Tim.'

'None.'

'So we end up looking stupid.'

'No, Tim dear; I phoned them all again this morning. Everyone's fighting fit and,' said Mother with a note of satisfaction, 'they all seem to think we are very caring; ... and you did, at least, do one good thing last night.'

'What was that?'

'Your little white lie; but it has left me feeling rather guilty.'


The "Sitting Duck" was a low cottage with a licence. Its proprietor, an elderly and taciturn Irishman of uncertain background, served, in his own time, from a bar made of driftwood. Warm beer came from wooden barrels. Dusty fishing nets, full of flotsam and jetsam, bits of boats, oars, sea shells and bright mooring buoys performed the office of a ceiling, the place being otherwise open to its rafters. The only building at the end of a remote peninsula its approach from the wider world was a narrow, pothole ridden lane which crossed wild, windblown fields with low hedges; then wound down a steep cwm of stunted oak trees, their crowns tattered and bent away from the westerly gales. Where the lane ended The Duck stood alone above a small beach of sand and shingle from which the sea stretched clear away to the West. These advantages, its elastic hours and the feeling that one was separated from the lets and hindrances of the modern world, had made the place a favourite summer watering hole for Tim and his friends. The winter was another matter. The brook from the cwm became a raging torrent and The Duck suffered from its proximity to the sea – occasionally flooded when tides were high and waves were running strong behind a sou-westerly wind. ...

With enough beer inside him Tim could imagine its history – dark figures rolling barrels of brandy up the shingle and strapping panniers of tobacco to ponies in the small hours. Now its only patrons were a faithful band of regulars, a few well spoken Englishmen who would come and go and about whom one knew little; and themselves. ... Tim had come to recognise his moments of loneliness in a crowd. Such standing apart came with a strange satisfaction; that of an observer freed from the constraints of conversation. ... He looked about him. Sophie and Francesca were perched on the sofa with fraying edges and which dipped in the middle. The others were at the bar; Friedrich and Camilla in loud conversation. They were drawing hostile glances from a cluster of locals gathered in the far corner ...

Tim felt a hand on his shoulder. ... 'It was hard on you last night; all that coming out,' whispered James.

'Well it did; and I got drunk, apparently.'

'Best thing. ... Have you heard any more from that lady?'

'No; not a thing; ... like it never happened.'

'Just as well.'

'When I left I did ask her if we could meet again.'

'What did she say?'

'Nothing; just shook her head; tears in her eyes. ... I wish I knew why. She's left me suspended; feeling a complete failure. ... Now I've met a girl who doesn't even know I'm interested in her and I don't know what to do about it. I can't get what happened out of my head ... and I don't want it to go wrong again. ... It's a mess.'

'You'll have to forget her, Tim.'

'We can't sit there any more,' cried Sophie, pushing between them, patting down her slacks. 'It's damp and the springs are poking my bum!' ... Sophie sniffed, leaned forward and sniffed again at Tim's jacket. 'I thought so. Why are you smelling of perfume, Tim? ... It's a bit stale but it could be Chanel or something just as good.'

'Perhaps he's been hugging his landlady,' said Francesca, laughing.

'You haven't seen her, Fran,' said Sophie, pushing her glass at Tim. 'Are you going to buy us a cider then?'

'My round,' said James, taking their glasses. ...

'Tim; ... a word;' ... Rhyd was beckoning from the bar. Tim hastily joined him, grateful of the opportunity to escape further inquisition. ...

'What the hell was going on last night; your "bruder" or whoever he is instructing everyone to be sick?'

'It's a long story,' sighed Tim; 'with a dead cat at the end of it.'

'Mother was past caring but he scared the pants off my Dad which is more than his fellow countrymen did on the battlefield.'

'Do you think I should ask him to keep his voice down?'

'Who?'

'Friedrich.'

'No; leave him be.'

'I think he's annoying them … over there.'

'They'll soon soften.' …

Tim knew that Rhyd was right for this was the demi-world of The Duck; the locals looking shifty; sizing up their occasional visitors; monitoring accents and conversation until the balm of alcohol dissolved the barriers of suspicion and envy. There had been wild nights in this place; some with cheeky girls Mother would not have approved of; a letting go; a joining of cultures; an abolition of social boundaries which, in the searching light of day, had inevitably returned. …

'He's popular with the women,' continued Rhyd, his attention drawn to Friedrich and Camilla who had moved to the far end of the bar. …'Do you think he's trying to run off with my sister?'…

The combination of his velvet gear, his sandals, his blonde hair drawn back and tied in Sophie's black bow made him look dashing in some inexplicable way. Tim was beginning to feel envious. May'be women thought he was boring, safe; too conventional. …May'be that had been the problem with Julia.

'Tell you what,' continued Rhyd, 'when I get back to Oxford I'm going shopping.'

'For what?'

'Jacket and trousers; just like his. … I reckon it's important they don't match; and, may'be, I'll let my hair grow a bit.'

'Your father wouldn't like it.'

'He'll have to lump it. … Tim I need a word with you … outside.' …

Rhyd stretched out on the insubstantial wooden bench parked against the white-washed wall and swigged at his pint. 'My Dad insists that all this is kept secret.'

'What secret?'

'He reckons that what your father did deserves a medal.'

'From whom? …He didn't die in a battle or anything.'

'Oddly, from the German government; … for saving one of their own. … Now this is the tricky bit. My Dad is very anxious not to upset your mother by raising it with her. He thinks that you should make the decision whether or not to take this any further … and keep your mouth shut. You see if Jerry decided not to award a medal where would that leave her?'

'Who approaches them?'

'My Dad, of course; he's got contacts in the War Office and they've got contacts over there.'…

Tim groped for a cigarette and lit it. … The sun was close to setting over a rare, cloudless horizon. A massive ball of fire, magnified and distorted by the earth's atmosphere, its dying light had become a gold and silver pathway over the flat calm of the sea. … 'Tell your Dad to go ahead.'

'OK; … one more question. Was he worth it?'

'Who?'

'Friedrich, of course,' said Rhyd, with a mischievous grin.

'How the hell am I supposed to answer that?'

'You'd better come in quick.' James was calling from the doorway. 'Friedrich's buying everyone a beer.'

Rhyd stood up and drained his glass.'What; … everybody; including the locals?'

'Yes; the whole pub,' said James, joining them. 'He says it's to further world peace; … and, when we've finished here, he wants us to go back to Tim's to finish his bottle of Schnapps.'

'Well,' cried Rhyd, heading for the door, 'I take it all back, Tim and I won't say no to world peace either; particularly if there's a free beer in it. Come on….'

# CHAPTER 14

Tim had been anxiously awaiting the day of the sale. He wanted a second chance with Fflur although the lingering memory of Julia had left him faint hearted. … He started at seven, after an early breakfast with Geraint. He wanted to be the first to arrive. As he drew into the yard he was hoping that she would be there. He was not disappointed. She and a farmhand were herding cattle across the yard. She turned briefly to watch him park. He rolled down his window, wanting to greet her in Welsh but she got in first. 'That's one thing we've got in common,' she shouted; 'a Morris Minor.' …

The selling of pedigree cattle was to be from a farm trailer to ensure that the auctioneer had a commanding view of bidders now cramming around a large ring which had been formed in temporary fencing at the centre of the farmyard. The proceedings began with an introduction by Mr Jenkin-Davies, a lean man standing next to Boz and taller than him, with an aquiline nose and thinning, black hair silvering at the edges. The firm's senior partner, his words were normally few and measured; his judgement, according to Teg, was universally trusted; his opinion and dry wit could, according to Boz, settle the bickering of implacable foes. An Olympian figure, inhabiting an office on the first floor with his two secretaries, Tim knew him to be kind and attentive – from time to time tactfully enquiring about his progress. ... The huge crowd listened in respectful silence as he delivered his speech in clearly spoken Welsh. Tim was pleased that he could now catch certain words and phrases; clues to the summing up of a good man's work of a lifetime. Standing upon the trailer as the flow of words rose and fell in the morning air he thought he could see a few in the crowd close to tears. This, then, was nigh on poetry; not the stuff that sometimes entered his head but the poetry of life itself. ...

By midday Boz had disposed of all the livestock. Teg had carried the bulk of the clerking, assisted for short spells by Tim. These he had perversely enjoyed in that he could stand close to Fflur, the keeper of the second book. He stood taller than her but not by much. She had exchanged her dungarees and overalls for loose fitting blue slacks, neatly tucked into wellington boots. In the increasing heat of the day she had removed her woollen cardigan and stood in a pretty white blouse with a high collar. He could inhale her perfume; its sweet, exotic scent a strange contrast to the ammoniac smells of the farmyard. They had said little to one another but she had helped him with the names of some of the local buyers.

The lunch for the auctioneers was a grand affair in the dining room of the farmhouse. The Minister of the family's chapel and their solicitor were guests at the meal of home grown beef and vegetables, followed by apple tart and custard – delivered by the tenant's wife and a bevy of other women, including Fflur, from a steaming kitchen across the hall. Tim was nervous; his stomach shrinking in the face of so much

189

food and in anticipation of his forthcoming public perform-ance. He had never sold machinery or furniture and had no idea of its value. Teg had elected to be his clerk and had promised to note suggested prices on the sale sheets for him to consult as he went but this would be selling to an unfa-miliar crowd in the open air. If he made a mess of it; if his voice gave out he would look a fool in front of Fflur and that would be that. …

The sale of the small machinery and implements was to be conducted from a cart towed from lot to lot in a nearby field. Tim's heart was pounding and his mouth was dry as he stood with Teg and Fflur. He looked about him. The large and cheerful crowd of the morning had diminished into small groups of crafty, knavish-looking men – eying him curiously; sizing up his inexperience in anticipation of bargains at the end of the sale. He had barely opened his mouth when one of them shouted in English. 'Just what we need; a posh Eng-lish boy to sell the glo man!'

Tim turned desperately to Fflur amid the laughter. 'What's glo man?'

'Coal dust; … leftovers,' she muttered; then turned to ad-dress the crowd in Welsh, sounding like a politician at the hustings. When she had finished the laughter had been si-lenced.

'What did you say to them?' whispered Tim, feeling emas-culated.

'I told them to shut up,' said Fflur, under her breath; 'that you were learning to be an auctioneer and learning Welsh at the same time and to give you a chance.'

The sale proceeded without further interruption. Tim reckoned that Fflur's intervention had intimidated the unruly and gained him some sympathy. He was beginning to feel confident; his voice deepening; resonating in the still, September air. Prices were not far away from Teg's estimates. When he got to the household furniture he was beginning to enjoy himself. Some women had joined the crowd. One of them, standing at the back, had been bidding for a bed against a man who turned out to be her husband. When this was discovered the crowd was in uproar. Tim offered to take her bids back but she waved him on, laughing with the rest. ... They had reached the last lot of the sale when Teg gestured him to stop. He was studying the horizon; his eyes screwed up against the sunlight. ... There was a movement there; a shimmering in the heat of the afternoon which, gradually, resolved into a large Jag being driven fast, lurching and bouncing over the uneven pasture. ....

'There he is,' said Teg, with a look of triumph. 'I wondered where he had got to.'

'Who's he?' asked Tim, wondering why his audience had turned its back on him to watch the approaching car.

'A wealthy man, Mr Tim – in a big way with business and he's got a large farm over there,' whispered Teg; ... 'I think he's come to buy.'

'But he's too late, Teg.'

'No he is not, Mr Tim,' said Teg happily, pointing at the last lot.

'But it's a commode! He can't possibly want that!'

'Wait and see, Mr Tim; wait and see,' said Teg with grim

satisfaction as the Jag skidded to a halt. A large man, his round face flushed, breathless and perspiring, leapt out of the car and ran towards the crowd, shouting at them in Welsh. He came to the cart, looked up at Tim and gasped – 'Am I too late?'

'No,' said Tim; 'we've got one more lot.'

'Which one?'

'That,' said Tim, unable to suppress a grin and pointing at the commode.

'I'll give you five quid for it,' muttered the man, desperately; 'it's a hell of a price for a sharp tap.'

'What's a sharp tap?' asked Tim.

'To knock it down quickly,' the man whispered impatiently.

'Six pounds!' The bid came from the crowd which had exploded into laughter.

'Seven,' the man shouted, looking put out.

'I thought that you already had an indoor toilet, Glyndwr,' shouted a man from the back. The comedy continued as the bidding went on, the man's expression fixed in the half smile of one who is resigned to his fate and knows that he should be seen to be making light of it in front of his peers. Finally the men allowed him to have the commode when the bidding reached twenty pounds; ten times its worth according to Teg who was evidently overjoyed at the result. Tim, still puzzled at his success with the commode, turned to Fflur who was recording the transaction and whispered. 'Why did he pay such a price?'

Fflur looked up from her book. He noticed that her eyes were aquamarine, almond shaped, vital; her long lashes batting at him. 'Don't be silly, Tim,' she exclaimed, 'he had to get his name on the book, don't you see?'

Tim had quickened at her mention of his Christian name. Now she was staring at him – bright with mockery; her lips parted, teasing; waiting for his response.

'*Fflur, is that your new boyfriend?*'.

'*Shut your mouth,*' snapped Fflur, glaring at a man who winked at her and disappeared into a group of others now preparing to leave.

Tim was feeling apprehensive. 'What was he saying?'

'Never you mind.'

'Mr Auctioneer!' The man who had bought the commode and who had since been in apparently friendly conversation with some of the men who had been mocking him, was shouting at Tim and pointing at his purchase – gesturing it away with the palms of his hands. 'I am going to pay my bill now,' he continued, 'but I will not be taking this with me. Anybody can have it as a gift. Do you hear?'

'He's making a show of not taking it,' whispered Fflur, who waved back at the man in acknowledgement.

'I've got a van here,' yelled one of the departing men, in English; 'I can deliver it right to your front door, Glyndwr. I'm sure your Mrs will be very pleased.'

'Bugger off, Willie!' shouted the man as he heaved himself into his car and drove away. ...

Returning from the field of his triumph Tim was met on the farmyard by the Brig, holding a plan. 'You've finished?'

'Yes sir; I think it went quite well.'

'Good; then there's another job for you to do; and you

can blame Captain Thomas for this. He thinks that the boundaries of the land need checking and he's suggested you; thinks that someone may be nibbling away at some woodland at the far end; that it'll be good experience for you; and I agree if only for the reason that I damned well don't want to do it myself. You should start now but be sure to meet me back here at eighteen hundred hours. If there's been any trespass I need to speak with the tenant right away. The last thing we want is adverse possession issues on a change of tenancy.'

'Yes I see, sir,' said Tim, swallowing hard in his disappointment at missing out on the post sale celebrations and a further opportunity to be with Fflur. He was wondering why Boz had landed him with this burden. …

'It's very important,' the Brig continued, 'that we have boundaries crystal clear in advance of a new tenancy and no hanky-panky on either side.' The Brig paused, looking about him. 'There's another thing. Captain Thomas says you should take somebody with you; someone who knows the place backwards. … It's clearly impossible to involve the tenant or his wife right now; but what about the daughter?' …

They were following the course of a slow moving brook which, according to the plan, formed the entire western boundary. Fflur was moving briskly; keeping ahead. Tim was admiring her long, chestnut hair, secured by a tortoiseshell barrette and hanging almost to the small of her back. He could see fleeting suggestions of her neat, firm curvature as she walked with the confidence of one who knows intimately the territory of her childhood. She had willingly come with him but her continuing silence was unnerving. …

'I hear you have a place in Aberystwyth,' said Tim, desperate to start a conversation; any conversation.

'So what,' said Fflur; 'It's a dump when it wants to be.' …

'Is it a flat or a house?'

'A what?'

'Your place?'

'I'm at the University.' Fflur stopped and turned to face him, her hands on her hips, her laughter abandoned and mocking; 'or do you think I'm too twp to be there? … Now I've made you blush.'

'I didn't go,' blurted Tim, catching up with her; angry with himself; knowing that he had reached a nadir in his efforts to impress her; that now there was nothing to be lost; that he might as well become a monk.

'Didn't go where?'

'Didn't go to university. … My father died in the war and my mother ran out of money. … I even had to leave school early.'

'Public school, I bet. I can tell it in your voice.'

'You don't like my voice?'

'Some of my friends wouldn't. They'd call it posh English, Tim. They'd think you were a nob.'

'Do you?'

'No, I don't; and my mam says you have lovely manners.' Fflur paused; 'and you got the better of that crowd in the end. That took some guts because they were all set to make fun of you; and you made them pay well for the glo man.'

'The leftovers?'

'There you are, Tim; you remembered. I'll make a Welshman out of you yet.' …

As they walked on together her hand slipped past the crook of his elbow, quickening him. He felt its warmth; clasped its softness in his as their fingers interlocked. Their hands parted as they came to a stile leading into a wood. Tim, silently cursing the interruption, stepped forward; then hesitated, his heart pounding; desperately reaching for words which would not come. He felt her arms encircle his waist, gripping him tight; then her hands reaching down to his thighs, the soft wetness of her lips on the back of his neck, the sweetness of her perfume, her breath in his hair. …

The accuracy of the plan had ceased to matter to Tim as they made their way back to the farmyard. Now Fflur was talking, her words pouring out; telling him she was an only child, where her parents were going to live; what she was doing at University; her campaigning for the Welsh language. Tim did not speak. They came to a pond, its surface a mirror to an apricot sky and the tree which overhung it. There they stood in silence, hand in hand, looking at their reflections; then turned to kiss. …

Back on the farmyard the Brig was beckoning and pointing at his watch. 'I thought I told you to report back by eighteen hundred hours, Barrington-Lewis. You're late; twenty minutes late,' he bellowed. 'I've been standing here like an unwanted ornament wondering where the hell you'd got to.'

'There was a complication, sir,' said Tim, walking towards him, fighting the temptation to give way to helpless laughter.

'There better have been. I'll have you know I am not in the

habit of being kept waiting.' The Brig looked about him. 'It's too late now to discuss whatever complication you're talking about. You hold onto the plan and I'll expect your full report in the morning.' ...

That night Tim went up to his room in the wake of a few whiskies with Gramp. He went to his table and picked up the plan. He marked with a cross the place of his encounter with Fflur, smiling at the thought that the Brig had become the un-witting sponsor of the whole wonderful affair. He turned off the light and opened the window. In the spectral light of a quarter moon the farmyard lay still; the fields mysterious, quiet, somehow unfamiliar. ... There had been a sharpening of his senses. Gramp had noticed something about him; had been probing but Tim knew that what had happened with Fflur, his abandonment of the unwanted baggage of youth, could not be spoken of to anyone; not to James, not to Rhyd, not even to Mother. In the harlequin light of that wood, in one dazzling moment under the trees she had become the love of his life. Now the mention of her name, the very thought of her made his heart beat faster. ... He wondered whether this was how it had been with Father and Mother; how they were when the picture on the bedroom wall was taken; the secret yearnings that parents never imparted to their chil-dren; the mystery of their creation. ... He wondered how it was that a beautiful girl who had appeared to despise him, mock him even, could suddenly come to love him in such an abandoned and natural way because, surely, she had seduced him. She had been the one to find a place to lie down; she had encouraged him; led the way. ... Had she gathered him

197

as a trophy; a posh English boy for her Nationalist cause? …
He didn't think so. … He could remember the softness of her
voice, the private things she had whispered as she lay beside
him, the sun and the leaves making patterns on her back –
this Venus of the West who had mysteriously taken his hand
when all seemed lost; who had led him safely over the sea
of his uncertainty for now his memory of Julia carried no
pain; had resolved into an affection for an older woman who
had shown him the way of lovers and then vanished. …

In the morning Tim was summoned to the Brig's office as
soon as he arrived at 'reception.'. …

'You look pleased with yourself,' snapped the Brig, unfurl-
ing the plan which Tim had handed to him. 'Now I want your
explanation as to why you were so damned late and it had
better be a good one.'

'If you look at the plan, sir, at the piece of woodland in
the south-western corner, you'll see a cross.'

'What the hell does that mean?'

'The boundaries look secure, sir but, where I marked with
a cross, there appears to have been some disturbance.'

'What disturbance?'

'I don't really know for sure, sir. The undergrowth is flat-
tened; pressed down. I just wondered whether anyone had
been camping there.'

'Is that it? Were you keeping me waiting while you were
investigating a depression in the undergrowth?'

'It seemed a bit mysterious, sir,' said Tim, suppressing a
smile.

'It sounds like a complete waste of time. You must be either a fool or a very fussy person; and I wish you wouldn't look so smug.'

'Is that all, sir?'

'No; you know that information you were getting from the wife of the machine-buff fellow. I've looked at your plan again. It's cock and bull; quite useless; doesn't tell us any more than we know already. I can't imagine why she wanted to see you about it.'

'She was a bit vague, sir,' said Tim, biting his lip, knowing the extent of his invention.

'The woman's been on to me again. They want to do something with the house. ... I really wonder whether she was trying, in some way, to soften you up; get us to pay for the lot. ... In the circumstances I have reluctantly agreed that the Estate will make a contribution.'

'What are the circumstances, sir?'

'They want to divide a bedroom; make a smaller room for a baby.'

'A baby, sir?'

'Yes, a baby.'

'Do you want me to inspect, sir?'

'Don't be in such a hurry. The work they're proposing is internal; non-structural and there are more pressing things on our hands at the moment.'

In the drawing office Jim was on the phone and making notes. Tim sat at his desk, looking out of the window, his mind racing. He couldn't concentrate on the plan in front of him. Jim finished his call, came over and patted him on the shoulder. 'It's looking good so far. Just remember to leave enough circulation space between the yard and the parlour. ... You didn't have another roasting from the Brig, did you?'

'No, he seemed to be in quite a good mood; for him.'

'Did he mention the lady you went to see about boundaries?'

'Yes, he did.'

'Well, she and her husband have been scratching a living on that farm on the wrong side of Twll Hill ever since the war and now she's expecting her first child; – a miracle, I say, because she must be getting on. They've been trying for years, apparently.'

'How do you know?'

'She told me; first call I took this morning; very forthcoming and that's a change because she's always been a quiet one and a bit of a mystery if you should ask me. ... They want to make some alterations; prepare for the baby, you see. I passed her on to the Brig and, fair play, when he heard about her expecting, he agreed that the Estate should pay some of the cost. ... He's a good old boy, really; when it matters.'

Tim hesitated. 'When is she expecting?'

'She says around Christmas time. That'll be nice for them. ... I'll get us some tea.'

Tim remained at his desk. Outside a strong wind was disturbing the trees on the castle mound, ripping at leaves, blowing them down to the brown and turbulent waters of the Rhyw.